Seems Like This Road Goes On Forever

Seems Like This Road

New York

Goes On Forever

Jean Van Leeuwen

The Dial Press

Published by
The Dial Press
1 Dag Hammarskjold Plaza
New York, New York 10017

Copyright © 1979 by Jean Van Leeuwen
All rights reserved. Manufactured in the U.S.A.
Design by Atha Tehon
First printing

Library of Congress Cataloging in Publication Data
Van Leeuwen, Jean. Seems like this road goes on forever.
Summary: A 17-year-old minister's daughter who feels her
world is crashing down suffers an emotional breakdown that
eventually forces her to make some difficult decisions.
[1. Emotional problems—Fiction. 2. Family life—Fiction.
3. Christian life—Fiction] I. Title.
PZ7.V3273Se [Fic] 78-72201
ISBN 0-8037-7687-X

The author is grateful to Jill Paulk, psychotherapist at South Beach Psychiatric Center and advanced student at the National Institute for the Psychotherapies; Wayne A. Myers, M.D.; Mary Berman, M.D.; and members of the staff of Northern Westchester Hospital for their time, patience, and valuable advice.

To Phyllis
for her caring, encouragement,
and perception

Seems Like This Road Goes On Forever

1

Mary Alice lay with her eyes half closed looking at the curtains again. She had been looking at the curtains for three or four days now. Or perhaps it was three or four weeks. It was hard to be sure. Time had slowed down, come almost to a stop since she had been in this bed in this room. Where before days had had a definite shape, a start and finish, now the days and nights seemed to blur together to become all one day, or one night, unused, interminable. Sometimes she was aware of changes in the light behind the curtains which must be dusk or dawn, but she could not keep in mind for long which it was.

The curtains were blue and green, an abstract, vaguely Indian print, surprisingly vivid compared to everything else in the room, which was colorless, faded. Lying there with her eyes half closed, Mary Alice could see in them changing shapes and figures: now a prancing horse, now a lion with curling whiskers, now a rotund smiling Buddha. It was a game she remembered playing a long time ago, in a room with sunlight streaming through pink flowered curtains. She had been seven or eight then, and happy, and had found a whole family of kittens hidden in the flowers.

The memory made her mouth twitch, all the expression her face could manage now. Like the rest of her body it seemed frozen, remote, immobile. She felt that she was not really in her body and that her body was not in this room. Mary Alice was somewhere else, disconnected, untouched, peaceful, like the serene Buddha in the curtains.

She looked for him again but found instead a different face. Sharply curving eyebrows drawn down over staring eyes, a thin angry line of mouth. It reminded Mary Alice vaguely of something, someone she knew, perhaps, or had once known. She pushed the thought away, closing her eyes as the nurse came into the room.

The nurse was like the curtains, brisk and determinedly cheerful. She bustled in and out of the room constantly, bringing food trays and pitchers of ice water and little paper cups with pills in them. She talked all the time and did not seem to notice that Mary Alice never answered. Other people drifted in and out of the room too, though less often. Another nurse, stiff and starched. A thin gray man who appeared to be a doctor, since he paid a great deal of attention to the bandage on her head and to her right leg, raised in an odd steel contraption they referred to as "traction." Another younger doctor who came in and took X-ray pictures of her leg. Other people in uniforms with mysterious adjustments to make to the complicated arrangement of weights and pulleys that surrounded the bed. Her mother and father. And, once, her friend Katie, carrying a bunch of yellow flowers and looking scared. Mary Alice saw them all from a great distance, but except for a whispered "yes" or "no" when the doctor or nurse insisted, she spoke to none of them. Her thoughts did not form themselves into words, and even if they had, her mouth no longer seemed to possess the knack of speaking.

The nurse's rubber-soled shoes squeaked across the floor to the window. The shade was snapped up. Then the shoes strode back to stand beside the bed. A tray was set down purposefully, glasses clinking.

Mary Alice's eyes were closed now, her breathing light, as if she were lost in sleep. She waited for the footsteps to retreat, for the nurse to leave her alone. But instead the nurse attacked the bed. Mary Alice felt it begin to rise beneath her head, surging violently upward until it reached a sitting position, and she with it. It jerked to a stop.

Mary Alice opened her eyes. The nurse was standing at the foot of the bed looking pleased with herself, as if it were not just the bed she had wound up but Mary Alice herself.

"Well, it's high time you were awake. Lying around sleeping all day—what do you think this is, a hospital?"

The nurse fluttered around the bed, fussing with the dishes on the food tray, tucking a napkin into the top of Mary Alice's nightgown, chattering all the while as if to make sure she remained awake.

"Here you are, the chef's special for today: beef ragout. That's beef stew to you and me. And I can tell you it's better than most of his specials. I got you a nice big helping."

She wheeled the tray close to the bed, positioning it tight against Mary Alice's chest so she could not escape the sight and smell of it.

An aroma of gravy rose from the tray, bringing with it a sharp image of an assembly line of green-uniformed women pouring endless ladles of gravy over endless anonymous school lunches. Mary Alice's stomach gave a lurch and she turned her head away.

The nurse did not appear to notice.

"Now when I come back, I expect to find that all of this fabulous food has vanished into thin air. Otherwise I'll have to tell Dr. Weber that you've been giving Mrs.

Burns a hard time. And that is against hospital regula-
tions, he will tell you. Strictly forbidden."

The nurse bounced out of the room. As her footsteps
receded down the hall, Mary Alice's stomach slowly subsided. She felt spent. The nurse's visits always tired her
out, as if it were she, not the nurse, who had expended all
that energy.

She looked down to discover that the food tray was still
there. She surveyed it without interest. On a green-rimmed
dinner plate, a pile of shriveled yellowish peas. A mound
of noodles, gray, wormlike. On top of them, lumps of
something so terrible that it had to be hidden beneath a
blanket of dark brown gravy. On a small plate, precisely
centered, one round dinner roll, one pat of butter. And
lined up behind, a glass of grapefruit juice, a carton of
milk, and a dish of red Jell-O cut into squares and topped
with a tiny dab of something that looked like shaving
cream.

There was nothing here that she could eat. Since she
had been in this room, Mary Alice had felt no hunger.
She was hollow inside, but the feeling had nothing to do
with food. All the food in the hospital kitchen could not
fill that void. So she ate nothing.

Mary Alice sat rigidly just as the nurse had arranged
her, hands folded under the food tray. She made no move
to push the tray away. Instead she stared into the dish of
Jell-O. She saw it suddenly not as something to eat but as a
work of art. It seemed to her strangely beautiful, its cubes

so symmetrical, so perfectly arranged, so clear and shining. Looking at it, she felt she was experiencing the color red for the first time in her life. She gazed into the dish as into a vast endless pool. It was pure as nothing else was.

"Do you mind if I sit down?"

With difficulty Mary Alice forced her eyes out of the pool of red. There was someone standing next to the bed.

It was a woman. She could not remember having seen her before. She did not seem to be a doctor or a nurse, for she wore no uniform. She was smiling, but it was not a pasted-on hospital smile like the nurse's. Her mouth just seemed to have a natural upward curve.

Mary Alice said nothing.

After a moment the woman noiselessly moved a chair close to the bed and sat down.

"I hope you don't mind my visiting you," she said. "I am Dr. Nyquist." Her voice was like her smile, quiet, uninsistent, restful.

Mary Alice looked at her. She wondered if underneath all the equipment surrounding her leg some kind of complications had set in, requiring the services of a specialist.

The doctor looked back at Mary Alice, still smiling. Mary Alice was aware that her eyes were very blue.

"Dr. Weber asked me to stop in to see you," she said. "I am a psychologist. I work with young people at the college here in Munson. I am sorry to interrupt your dinner. Please go ahead and eat."

Mary Alice sat very still, her hands gripping each other under the food tray.

The doctor leaned back in her chair. It was impossible to guess her age. She had a young-old face, the skin smooth and unlined except at the corners of the eyes. Her hair, pulled back from her face, seemed equally blond and gray.

A minute passed.

"I understand that your head and your leg are coming along nicely. Do you have much pain now?"

Mary Alice thought about the question. It seemed to her that she had no more pain in her head or leg than in the rest of her body. Perhaps she had no pain at all. Or perhaps much pain. The question could not be answered.

The doctor sat quietly. She seemed to be waiting for something, but not pressing, as if she had plenty of time. Mary Alice noticed that her sweater and skirt matched the color of her hair. Even her clothes were muted, neutral.

Mary Alice felt that she too was waiting for something. She did not know what it was.

Then the doctor quietly slid back her chair and stood up.

"I must be going now," she said. "But I will come back in three or four days to see how you are coming along."

She stood for a moment, smiling, then walked soundlessly from the room.

Mary Alice remained motionless, her hands clasped tightly, the food tray still pressing against her chest. She stared at the chair in which the doctor had sat. It was empty now, uninhabited, yet it was as if she were still there. Her eyes, her voice, her presence, echoed in the room.

Mary Alice sat there and time passed, minutes or perhaps hours. The light faded slowly behind the curtains. With it the image of the doctor began to fade until at last it seemed that she had never been there. The room was as before. Mary Alice was aware of a feeling of relief.

The nurse came back then to take away the food tray, making disapproving clucking sounds about the untouched meal. It occurred to Mary Alice that what the nurse most resembled was a small fretful white hen. She pecked about the room, adjusting the bed, the lamps, the window shade, the bed again. In and out she went, endlessly busy, bringing the bedpan, still another pitcher of water, and finally the last pill of the day, a bright pink one.

The nurse held the glass of water and Mary Alice swallowed it obediently. She did not know what the pills were for: pain perhaps. But she always felt the same after taking them as before.

The nurse lowered the bed, straightened the sheets one final time.

"There now. I'm going to leave your reading lamp on in case you feel like looking at some of those magazines your mother brought. If you want anything later, you can call the night nurse. Sleep well."

Then, at last, she was gone.

The room was quiet, dark except for the circle of yellow light from the reading lamp that fell across the bed. On the other side of the room the armchairs and chest of drawers sat hunched in darkness, reassuring and at the same time vaguely sinister. A vase of tall white flowers threw a strange many-headed shadow on the wall.

Mary Alice lay still and looked into the darkness. Her eyes went to the curtains, and for a moment she thought she saw those staring eyes looking back at her. Then a breeze stirred the curtains and the image was gone.

From the hallway outside she was aware of the hospital's night sounds: a cart rolling by, a far-off telephone, a nurse's shoes squeaking past on some errand, a sudden laugh—or was it a cry? The sounds were somehow soothing.

Mary Alice closed her eyes and thought about nothing. Slowly she drifted into a half-sleep. As the days and nights had become blurred together, so had the line between sleeping and waking. She no longer sank into sleep but skimmed along its surface, remote from her surroundings yet never totally relinquishing her hold on them. She felt on guard against sleep. It was a pit she must not fall into.

And now Mary Alice was floating, adrift high in a bright blue sky. Around her, cotton clouds, fat and fine, moved slowly by. She was suspended in space and time, like a balloon escaped from earth. If she looked down, far far below, she could see the earth: a small round beautiful ball covered with green and yellow squares, brilliantly colored, perfectly formed.

From it rose the faint sound of voices. They seemed to be calling her. But Mary Alice could not make out what they were saying.

2

She was in a dark place. Alone. Traveling somewhere at great speed.

It appeared to be a space capsule. She was sitting in a space capsule enclosed by darkness. Speeding through endless silent space on her way to another planet.

Outside the window blurred shapes rushed by. She could not quite make out what they were. She rubbed her hand across the glass, but it would not clear.

There seemed to be a need to go faster. Now the shapes blurred together until they looked like silver lines on either side of her capsule. Stars—they must be stars, she thought. And went faster, leaving them behind.

She was streaking through space, herself a shooting star. It occurred to her that she did not know the name of the planet to which she was going. And she hadn't brought along any of those little plastic envelopes of food that space travelers were supposed to carry. She needed to talk to someone on the ground. She searched the instrument panel in front of her, but she could not find the right button. She had forgotten which button she was supposed to press to talk to Mission Control.

She was alone, and going faster.

Now her capsule suddenly began to spin. It wasn't supposed to do that. Around and around it went, making her dizzy. Frantically she started pushing all the buttons in front of her. But it was no use. The capsule kept spinning.

She was falling. She tried to hang on to something, to stay upright, but she could not. The space capsule was out of control. Something dreadful was going to happen.

Mary Alice woke up, her whole body shaking as if with a terrible chill.

3

The woman doctor came again. Mary Alice opened her eyes and found her sitting there with the same shadow of a smile, the same calm voice.

"How are you feeling today?"

When Mary Alice didn't answer, the doctor said quietly, "I understand that you are finding it difficult to talk now." She sat for a few minutes, filling up the emptiness, and then she went away. And came back again.

Mary Alice found her visits disturbing. There was something in her voice, her eyes, her stillness, that offered comfort. And yet Mary Alice was aware of danger. The doctor wanted something; her voice and her eyes probed, no matter how gently. Why didn't she leave her alone?

Mary Alice did not understand why they all would not leave her alone. She felt now that she had always been in this room, lying flat on her back, motionless, imprisoned in this steel cage they called traction. She could hardly remember if there had been a time before her being here. Nothing but the room seemed real. It had become pleasing to her: the squat scarred blond furniture, the cracks that snaked across the ceiling above her head, the curtains with their hidden surprises, the bed's gleaming metal poles and pulleys that reminded her of circus acrobats, the shallow contours of her own inanimate body beneath the white bedspread. The landscape was familiar, reassuring.

She thought of herself as a rock over which water flowed. Though waves beat unceasingly against it, the rock felt nothing. The waves washed over, leaving the rock as it was before: immovable, untouchable. It was a pleasant sensation.

It struck her as odd that others did not seem to understand what she had become, that they would not let her be what she had become. The nurse still came with her pills and ice water and trays of food, urging her to wake up, read a magazine, eat something. Sometimes she would sit next to the bed and lift spoonfuls of food to Mary

Alice's mouth, and then Mary Alice would chew and swallow it as if she were a baby. It seemed too much trouble to resist, or perhaps it was just that she had the habit of compliance, a habit too strong to break even now. But each bite of food lay in her stomach like a small sharp stone.

And her mother and father seemed always to be there. They would sit stiffly side by side in the two armchairs with the green seats, and though she knew them to be her parents, they seemed like strangers, someone else's visitors who had wandered into her room by mistake. A rather small woman with a trim figure and a pleasant face clutching a brown purse in her lap. Everything about her was tidy, well-organized: the small neat features, the short dark hair that fell into crisp, no-nonsense waves, the tailored knit dress. Her mouth smiled easily, yet in her eyes there was something not quite focused, something that would not hold still. Next to her a tall man in a dark blue suit, his large hands resting awkwardly on his knees. His body was lean, devoid of any fat. His face too had an austere look, the cheeks slightly sunken, the mouth a thin tight line, the graying hair combed straight back. But it was his eyes that dominated his face. They were pale blue and seemed to burn with some fierce inner fire. He looked like what he was: a man of God.

As soon as Mary Alice opened her eyes, her mother would start to talk.

"Oh, you're awake, Mary Alice. I'm glad. You sleep too much, you know. Dr. Weber says you don't need that much rest. Have you been doing the exercises he gave you for your other leg?"

Her father did not speak. But his eyes were focused on Mary Alice's face, troubled, troubling.

"So many of the church people have asked for you," her mother went on. "The Wilsons and the Nylanders and the Powells and Miss Hill and of course Mrs. Braxton. She has sent you a bunch of forsythia from her garden. Everyone has been so thoughtful."

Then she would begin to unpack the shopping bag next to her chair. It was a pink bag with black letters on the side, so elaborately flowing that they could hardly be read, advertising Pearl's Department Store.

"Here are the get-well cards that came today. And I brought you a summer nightgown—it's much too warm in this room for long sleeves. And your hairbrush and a mirror. Really, Mary Alice, you must do something with your hair. What will the doctor and nurses think?"

Her father's eyes continued to bore into Mary Alice, asking questions, as her mother talked obliviously on.

". . . so I told the nurse that you aren't used to this hospital food, and she said it would be all right if I brought you just a couple of slices of my banana bread. Oh, and I slipped in a few brownies too, since I was making them for the Women's League luncheon."

The eyes would not let Mary Alice go. They pierced through all layers of defense. Cold, unyielding, they stood in judgment over her. They were, she realized suddenly, the eyes she had seen in the curtains.

Involuntarily her hand rose to cover her own eyes.

"What is it, Mary Alice?" her mother asked. "Does your head ache? Oh, dear, I'm afraid we've stayed too long and tired you out."

She gathered herself to leave, sweeping papers into the wastebasket, tidying up the bedside table.

"Now tomorrow we're going to be terribly busy. I've got the Women's League luncheon, and your father has Men's Bible Study. And then there's the Friday Fellowship in the evening. But we'll try to stop in just for a few minutes. Mrs. Braxton said she'd be glad to stay with Julia any time we want to come to the hospital. She's been so sweet."

Carefully she folded up the empty shopping bag. "Well, good-bye, dear. Be sure to eat the banana bread while it's fresh."

Her father rose slowly to his feet. He stood there, a silent reproachful shadow looming over the bed. He appeared to be studying Mary Alice, as if she were some exceptionally intricate and elusive puzzle. Mary Alice did not look up at him, but she felt his presence like some other part of herself.

"Good-bye, Mary Alice," he would say at last, his voice low, lifeless. And he would turn to leave. Only once had he said anything more. He had leaned close, so close that she could not escape those eyes, boring relentlessly into her, threatening to engulf her.

"You are in our prayers," he had said. "Your mother and I pray for you every night."

And now her brother, Peter, sat in the same chair where her mother had sat, where the doctor had sat. He had come all the way home from college to see her, three hundred miles on the bus, and he had to go right back. Although he had just gotten off the bus, he looked as he always did: his dark curly hair neatly trimmed and combed, his clothes seemingly just pressed. He had not changed in the three years he had been away at college. He had not changed since he was six years old.

He smiled at her. "How are you doing, Linda Lovely?"

Only Peter called her that. He had given her the name one day when she was about thirteen and he had come upon her studying herself in her mother's full-length mirror. If anyone else had said it, Mary Alice would have felt they were laughing at her. But Peter had made her feel accepted, as if there was hope in what she saw in the mirror.

The memory of it, his smile, caused the weight to lift slightly from Mary Alice's body.

Now Peter was looking down at the left sleeve of his sweater, picking tiny balls of yellow wool from it with his right hand. His smile had faded. A small frown wrinkled the center of his forehead as it did whenever he was working on a problem. He was a solver of problems, a scientist. When he was seven or eight, he had known the names of all the dinosaurs and what they liked to eat. Now, in college, he was studying something called astrophysics.

Peter drew in a deep breath, as if making up his mind about something. "Mary Alice," he said, "you've gotten yourself into a real mess."

He looked up at her, his eyes grave behind his clear-rimmed glasses.

Mary Alice felt the weight settle down around her again. He was not going to leave her alone. Not even Peter.

Peter leaned forward, his frown deepening. But when he spoke, his voice was quiet, reasonable, as always. "Mary Alice, this is a serious situation. You have taken something—stolen something—from a store. The police know about it. You can imagine how Mother and Dad feel about that. Not only that, but you've wrecked Dad's car and put yourself in the hospital with a bump on the head and a broken leg. Not just a regular broken leg but a broken femur, which is going to keep you here five or six weeks. You're lucky you weren't killed. And now you lie here with nothing to say."

Mary Alice heard his words, but they seemed to have nothing to do with her. They washed harmlessly over her, leaving no mark. She looked down at the bottom of the bed, where her good foot stuck up under the bed-spread like a miniature mountain peak. She wondered if it was frozen that way forever. Experimentally she commanded her foot to move and was surprised to see it obey.

"Mary Alice, you have to listen. This is important. Please look at me."

There was something different in his voice. He sounded upset. Peter never got upset. She couldn't bear for him to be upset with her.

Obediently Mary Alice lifted her eyes. She willed herself to focus on his words and comprehend them. She fastened her eyes on his mouth, as if that might help.

"Mary Alice, please listen carefully. There is something you have to know. I have been talking to Mother and Dad on the telephone almost every night. They are very concerned about you. Really worried. Not just about what you did but about the way you are acting now—not eating, not talking, like you're in some kind of trance. They've been discussing it with Dr. Weber. He feels that you have had some kind of emotional breakdown. He wants to have you examined by a psychiatrist. When your leg is better, he is thinking of having you moved to another hospital for observation. A mental hospital, Mary Alice."

Mary Alice was aware of a strange tightness gathering inside her, forming itself into a hard knot in the pit of her stomach.

Peter went on, his voice quieter. "Mother and Dad aren't sure what to do. You know they don't believe in such things as emotional breakdowns and psychiatrists. According to them, it's all a matter of will power, pulling yourself up by your boot straps. Dad feels that you are going through some kind of spiritual crisis and that you can only be healed through prayer. And Mother thinks there is nothing wrong with you at all, it's just the shock of the accident and you'll be fine with rest and plenty of good home-cooked food. As she says, there have never been any mental problems in *our* family."

Peter wrinkled up his nose as he said this, just as he used to when he was little.

Mary Alice felt the tightness spreading upward, constricting her chest, her throat.

"Well, I finally convinced them to have Dr. Nyquist talk to you. Dr. Weber suggested her. She is a psychologist, but she also teaches at the college here in Munson, so Mother and Dad think of her as kind of a counselor. She has worked with a lot of young people, at Boston University before she came here. And the best part of it from Mother's point of view is that if you see her while you're in the hospital here in Munson, there isn't much chance of the congregation over in West Greenville hearing about it. The disgrace and shame of it all won't get out. The thing is, Mary Alice, that you've got to talk to this doctor. If you don't, I'm not sure what will happen."

Peter stopped talking. His right hand reached up and pushed his glasses back on his nose, then fell to his lap.

There was silence in the room.

Something—a sob, a scream—was building in Mary Alice's throat. She struggled to swallow it, keep it inside.

"Well, Mary Alice, what do you say?"

Peter was looking at her expectantly, hopefully.

She could not answer him. She could not look at him.

There was another minute of silence. Peter shifted in his chair. His hand reached over to the bed, hesitated, then came down over hers, enclosing it in warmth.

A long shudder ran through Mary Alice's body.

She looked up at him, opening her mouth to speak. But all that came out was a choking sound. She managed only to nod her head, then turned away.

And at last tears came.

4

It was moving day. They had just moved into their new house. Her mother was busy unpacking cartons in the kitchen. Mary Alice was trying to help, but her mother kept telling her not to touch the glasses, they might break, not to climb up on the stool, she might fall, not to touch the box with the number 19 in the corner until she finished the one numbered 18. Finally she said, "Mary Alice, I wish you would just go find something else to do until I finish in here. Then I'll come upstairs and try to find your crayons and coloring book."

Mary Alice picked up her teddy bear and wandered through the living room with boxes piled all over the place and their furniture pushed together in a corner not looking at all like it used to look in the old house, and she thought that this house could never be their home.

She went outside and sat down on the front steps, holding her bear. It was a hot afternoon. The street was quiet. She could hear the splashing sound of a sprinkler turning around and around in the yard next door. The next-door lawn was bright green with new grass. Their own lawn had a dried-up brownish appearance and had not been mowed for a long time.

Mary Alice looked up and down the street, trying to guess which houses might have children living in them. On each side of their house were old people, but the big gray house across the street looked promising. There were two bicycles tipped over in the driveway, and the front yard was strewn with toys: trucks, guns, a wagon, a couple of baseball gloves. Boys, thought Mary Alice. Big boys.

Just as she thought it, two boys came around from the back of the house. They were big, almost as big as Peter, and they both had reddish-blond hair and wore cut-off jeans and no shirts. They might have been twins, but one looked a little bigger than the other. They picked up the baseball gloves and started throwing a ball back and forth. They threw hard, and whenever one of them missed, the other laughed. They did not look across the street.

Mary Alice pretended not to be watching them either. She looked down the street for her father's car. Her father and Peter had gone to the hardware store.

In a few minutes the front door of the gray house opened and another boy came out. He was smaller than Mary Alice, about three or four. He was also wearing shorts and no shirt and a red baseball hat that was too big and came down over his eyes. He wanted to play ball too, but the big boys wouldn't let him. He kept trying to catch the ball and getting in their way, and finally the big boys threw down their gloves and tossed him the ball. Then they got on their bikes and coasted down the driveway.

Mary Alice kept her eyes down. She studied an ant that was running along the step between her feet, apparently in a great hurry to get somewhere. When she looked up again, the boys were way down at the end of the street. She saw them turn around and come back, fooling around, cutting in front of each other, riding no-hands. She looked down again at the ant. It was trying frantically to figure out how to get around her left foot. She watched its confusion for a minute and then, feeling sorry for it, moved her foot. When she looked up this time, the boys were on the sidewalk in front of her house.

"Hi," said the bigger one. His thin face had the most freckles she had ever seen, and he was chewing gum very hard.

"Hi," said Mary Alice.

"We saw you moving in yesterday," he said. "You sure have a lot of stuff."

Mary Alice didn't know what to say to that. She nodded.

The smaller boy blew out a pink bubble that got bigger and bigger until it covered most of his face. When it finally popped, he pushed the gum back in his mouth with a dirty finger and said, "We thought we saw a boy over here before. You got a brother?"

Mary Alice nodded again. "He's not home now. His name is Peter. He's nine."

The bigger boy got off his bike and leaned it against a tree. He came up the walk, followed by the smaller one.

"I'm Ralph," he said, sitting down. "This is Eddie. And that little creep over there is Jimmy." He shook his head in disgust. "You can't get away from that kid. He's like a leech."

Mary Alice saw that the little boy was crossing the street toward them, carrying a ball and glove.

"My name is Mary Alice," she said.

Eddie dug deep into his pocket and came out with a wrinkled package of bubble gum. He unwrapped it, broke off a piece, and added it to what was already in his mouth. "Want some?" he offered.

Mary Alice took a piece. "Thank you," she said.

"Me too." Jimmy appeared next to Eddie, his hand outstretched.

"Not you," said Eddie, holding the gum out of his reach. "You already had half the package."

"Just one more piece," begged Jimmy. Mary Alice saw that his face under the baseball hat was a smaller copy of Ralph's.

"Oh, okay," said Eddie. He broke off a piece of gum and handed it to Jimmy. "But that's all you get. All day."

Jimmy sat down on the step below Mary Alice and started chewing, looking totally contented.

Mary Alice put her gum in her mouth too. It felt stiff at first, and it had a strange taste, somewhere between strawberry and banana. But it didn't matter. The taste was just something you had to get over with before you got to the good part, the bubble blowing.

"Where'd you move here from?" asked Ralph after a minute.

"Glenwood," said Mary Alice.

Ralph shook his head. "Never been there."

Eddie blew another one of his giant bubbles. "When's your brother coming back anyway?"

"Soon," said Mary Alice. "He just went to the store with my father."

"We'll wait," said Ralph.

They sat on the steps, blowing bubbles, not talking. Mary Alice tried to blow one as big as Eddie's, but she couldn't—they kept popping. She guessed it was because she didn't have as much gum as he did, and thought about asking him for another piece. But she didn't. She felt pleased to be sitting there surrounded by her three new friends. She was afraid somehow of breaking the spell.

"Hey," said Ralph suddenly. "What's that you've got there?"

"What?" asked Mary Alice.

Ralph reached out a finger and touched her teddy bear. "This."

"Oh," said Mary Alice, "that's just my bear."

"Just your bear—why, it looks like a big old grizzly to me. Let me see that."

Reluctantly Mary Alice handed him her bear.

"Hey, look at that, it *is* a grizzly bear. And a mean one too. Listen to him roar." Ralph thrust the bear suddenly at Jimmy, and the little boy jumped.

Ralph laughed. "He sure is a mean one. But wait a minute. Eddie, you know what? There's something wrong with this girl's bear. Do you know that this bear doesn't have a belly button?"

Eddie stopped in the middle of a bubble. "You must be kidding. Let me look at that bear."

Ralph tossed him the teddy bear.

Eddie ran his fingers through the fur on the bear's stomach. "You're right," he said. "No belly button. This is very bad."

"It's all right," said Mary Alice. "I don't care if he doesn't have a belly button. Let me have my bear back."

Ralph shook his head. "We can't do that. We're going to have to operate on this bear. Have you got your instruments, Eddie?"

Eddie patted his pocket. "Right here."

"Come on then," said Ralph, standing up.

"Where are you going?" asked Mary Alice.

"You stay here," said Ralph. "Don't worry, you'll get your bear back. Just as soon as we fix him up."

The two boys walked over to the side of the house, where a tall hedge separated Mary Alice's yard from the yard next door. They knelt down, their backs to her.

Mary Alice couldn't see what they were doing. She wanted to get off the steps and look, but she was afraid to. She looked at Jimmy. He was busy rolling his ball along the step and then throwing the glove at it to stop it. He didn't seem aware that anything was happening.

The two boys were whispering, their heads close together. Ralph had a stick in his hand. Eddie took something out of his pocket and handed it to him. There was more whispering and nudging. A minute later Mary Alice smelled something burning.

"My bear!" She ran across the yard. "What did you do to my bear?"

The boys stood up. They were both grinning. "We just gave him a belly button like we said," said Ralph.

Her bear was lying face down in the dirt. Mary Alice turned him over. In the middle of his stomach was a gaping hole, from which a wad of white stuffing protruded. All around the hole his fur was scorched black.

"We did it with this. See?" Eddie was holding a stick, the end of it still smoking.

Mary Alice picked up her bear. Very carefully she pushed the stuffing back into the hole. She tried to rub the black from his fur with her finger, but it wouldn't come out.

"What's the matter, don't you like his belly button?" asked Ralph, his eyes wide, innocent. "We were just trying to fix him up for you."

Mary Alice couldn't answer. She held her bear tightly. Tears filled her eyes, then spilled slowly down her cheeks.

"What are you doing to my sister?"

Peter was suddenly standing there. Big Peter, looking even bigger in his football shirt. Looking tough even, with a scowl on his usually mild face.

"What's going on here? You better leave my sister alone."

It was all right. Peter was there.

5

"Good morning, Mary Alice."

It was early, just past breakfast. The tray—untouched—still sat next to the bed.

Mary Alice was not ready for the doctor. And there was the way she looked. Her cheeks were flushed pink, her eyes bright, their color made more vivid by the blue wool suit she wore. She seemed aglow with health, a walking admonishment to those who lacked her apparent mastery of life.

"It seems that spring is not quite here yet after all. It's a little nippy this morning. But beautiful." She rubbed her arms as if to warm them, smiling.

Mary Alice felt herself turning back into stone. It had been foolish to think she might be able to talk to this doctor. Foolish to think she could talk at all.

Dr. Nyquist moved the armchair into the position she seemed to prefer, exactly at the middle of the bed but turned slightly toward its head. She sat down, unbuttoning her jacket, crossing her legs. Her face still wore the trace of a smile, as if she possessed so much inner happiness that it could not all be contained within her.

Really, thought Mary Alice, anyone who looked like that should not be allowed inside a hospital.

The doctor's smile faded almost imperceptibly, and her face again took on that expression of repose, serene, accepting. She leaned back in her chair.

"Now," she said in her soft voice, as if thinking out loud, "where shall we begin?"

Mary Alice waited for the doctor to answer the question. She certainly was not going to help her.

"I think," Dr. Nyquist began slowly, her eyes on Mary Alice's face, "that you are wondering if you can talk to me. If you can trust me. After all, you don't know me. And it wasn't you but your parents who asked me to come to see you. You're probably concerned about what I will tell them about our meetings, how much of what you say to me will be repeated to them."

She leaned forward slightly. Her eyes held Mary Alice's,

steady, intent, terribly blue. They reminded Mary Alice of her father's eyes, but there was something different in them. They seemed to be offering something. Mary Alice was not sure she was ready to accept it.

"I will promise you two things," the doctor went on, her voice still quiet. "Nothing that we say to each other in this room will ever go outside it. Your parents won't know what we talk about. Our conversations will be between the two of us—no one else. And we won't talk about anything until you feel ready to talk about it. There's no hurry. We'll have as much time as you need."

She paused as if to give Mary Alice time to consider her words.

"In return I would like you to promise me one thing. I want you to try to tell me as many of your thoughts as you can—even those that may frighten you. They won't be so frightening when they are shared, you'll see."

She smiled again suddenly. "Well, Mary Alice, how would that be as a bargain? Will you let us try?"

There was something conspiratorial in her smile, rather like Mary Alice's friend Katie when she was plotting some secret to be kept from her little sister. Mary Alice wondered whether she could really trust this doctor—or whether she was about to fall into some kind of trap.

Nevertheless she found herself nodding her head.

"Good," said the doctor. She leaned back again, looking pleased. "While you are in the hospital, we will meet two or three times a week—we'll talk about what is most helpful for you. And then we'll see what you might want to do after you leave the hospital. The first thing I would like to do is become a little better acquainted. Most of what I know about Mary Alice Fletcher is from these hospital forms, and they don't tell me much."

Mary Alice felt the knot beginning to form again in her stomach, pulling her whole body taut. The doctor was going to ask questions. She was not ready for questions. It was a mistake.

"Suppose I start by telling you what I do know. After that you can fill in the blank spaces for me."

Dr. Nyquist's voice was matter-of-fact, cheerful, as if this were some kind of harmless game.

"Let me see. I know that you were born in Philadelphia, Pennsylvania, and that you are seventeen. Your birthday is November 24, so that would make you a senior in high school. Your parents' names are John and Louise Fletcher. You have a brother, Peter, who is twenty-one, and a sister, Julia, who is nine."

Little by little the tautness began to leave Mary Alice's body. She listened to the doctor's voice, feeling that she was hearing a story about someone else, a person she did not know.

"You live in West Greenville, where your father is pastor of the First Reformed Church. I believe you have lived there about four years?"

It was easy to remember. They had moved to West Greenville the summer before her freshman year. Mary Alice nodded.

"I don't know West Greenville very well," said the

doctor. "But I've passed through it once or twice on my way to Hooten Falls. That's where the glove factory used to be, isn't it?"

Mary Alice nodded again. She tried to think about the town where she lived, where she had once lived. West Greenville. The name seemed to conjure up no images.

"It seemed like a pretty town. Very small, I remember."

Now an image drifted into Mary Alice's mind, clear as a postcard. It was a view of downtown West Greenville, looking north on Main Street. There was Bob's Full-Service Gas Station in the foreground and next to it the volunteer fire department, newly painted yellow, and then the dark, vacant building where the A&P used to be before it moved out to the shopping center. Across from that the drugstore and the five-and-ten and the red brick bank and the bright display-filled windows of Pearl's Department Store.

"Do you like living there?"

It was a question Mary Alice had never asked herself. She lived in West Greenville because that was where her father had taken them. It was where God needed him, he had said, his eyes glittering with excitement when he told them about the move. Where His work was. Mary Alice had accepted the town as she had accepted other towns before it. Without comment.

It occurred to her now that she disliked West Greenville. The thought startled her. Disliking things was frowned upon in her parents' house. "Now, Mary Alice, you don't really," her mother always said.

All the same, Mary Alice felt it was true. Slowly she shook her head.

Dr. Nyquist did not seem surprised. "Why do you think you feel that way?" she asked.

Now a series of images began flooding into Mary Alice's consciousness. The old houses on High Street, tall, dignified, surrounded by porches and the leafy arms of giant trees. The new houses on the edge of town, neat, compact, surrounded by tricycles. The brick factory next to the river, once the reason for the town's existence, now silently crumbling, forgotten. The new A&P with its vast echoing corridors of food, overwhelming in size, brightness, choices. The car wash. The drive-in bank. The farm machinery store with its bright new machines lined up in front. Rick's Tavern, dark, cozy-looking, with its red beer sign beckoning in the window and cars parked outside at all times of the day and night. Her father's church, white, rectangular, without steeple or bell or stained-glass windows like the Methodist Church, unprepossessing, unprosperous.

The images tumbled one on top of another, lacking coherence, canceling one another out. Mary Alice tried to find in them a pattern, an explanation, but she could not. She shook her head, confused.

"Perhaps," suggested Dr. Nyquist mildly, "it is not really the town that you dislike." She leaned forward slightly, her chin resting on her fingertips. "Perhaps this feeling has to do with things that have happened to you since moving to West Greenville. It might be helpful for you to tell me a little bit about the town. About your life there."

Your life there. The words sounded strange to Mary Alice. Inappropriate somehow. She looked up at the ceiling, trying to think of what could be said about her life.

Her eyes traced the shape of the crack in the plaster above her head. It wound around in an S shape, and from it spread many smaller cracks, like branches of a tree. They wandered off in different directions, starting out well enough but quickly petering out, going nowhere. Like her life.

Mary Alice closed her eyes.

"Are you tired?" asked the doctor, sounding concerned.

Mary Alice was aware of being very tired. So tired that she longed to remain with her eyes closed, letting sleep enfold her like a dark warm blanket. But she was also aware now that there was something she had to tell the doctor. Something that the doctor did not understand.

Mary Alice opened her eyes. The doctor was smiling at her again, that smile that seemed to offer so much.

"There is nothing to talk about," said Mary Alice. She was surprised to find that her voice was calm, clear, normal-sounding, as if she had just spoken a few minutes ago, not days or perhaps weeks before. "I have had no life."

6

They were driving along a highway at night, her mother and father in the front seat, she and Peter in the back, going home from somewhere.

Mary Alice liked to ride in the car, especially at night. She liked the soft murmuring sounds of the tires on the road, her mother and father talking quietly in the front seat. She liked the way the car headlights pierced through the darkness, lighting their way through the unknown countryside. She liked the feeling of going somewhere when other people were home doing the dishes and getting ready for bed.

Peter always went right to sleep, leaving Mary Alice alone, and she liked that too. She would press her face against the window, looking up sideways to see if she could find the moon. She peered into the dark woods, trying to imagine what the deer and raccoons and other animals who lived there were doing, hidden by the night. When they passed a lighted house she would try to look inside, hoping to catch a glimpse, however fleeting, of someone else's life. It was always too quick, she could never quite capture it, but still she tried. And when they encountered another car along the road, she wondered who the people inside could be and what they were doing out so late.

They drove and they drove and now it seemed that there were no other cars on the road except them. The houses they passed were dark, the people sleeping. The voices from the front seat grew still. Her mother and father had run out of conversation.

The night itself seemed darker. Mary Alice saw that the moon had gone down.

And then her mother said, "It seems to me that this road goes on forever."

Her father did not reply. The words hung in the air.

Mary Alice thought about how awful it would be if her mother were right. If the road kept on going and it was always dark and there was no exit, no way to get to where they were going.

And then she had another thought. She thought that maybe she would like it if the road went on forever.

7

"I've been thinking about what you said at the end of our visit Tuesday. About your feeling that you have not had a life."

It was as if they had not been interrupted, as if two days had not passed since the doctor's last visit. For the first time Mary Alice had found herself aware of the passage of time. She saw that the hospital day arranged itself into a pattern: the taking of her temperature so early in the morning that it seemed like it was still night, the breakfast tray, the inspection of her leg by the gray doctor, the changing of the bed linen, the lunch tray, her parents' visit, the dinner tray. A series of small events surrounded by large empty spaces. She had begun to feel impatient for each event to be over so that the next could follow, so that the day would be finished, so Dr. Nyquist would come again. She had looked forward to the doctor's visit with an odd eagerness, as if something momentous would come of it. Now that she was here, so composed, asking more questions, Mary Alice was not sure why. She felt closed up again, unable to explain anything, unable even to speak.

"Can you tell me what you meant when you said that you have had no life? I want to be sure that I understand."

The doctor's eyes were so friendly, so encouraging. Why were her questions so difficult? Mary Alice tried to remember what had made her say such a thing.

"Do you mean that your life has been uneventful?"

Mary Alice nodded, grateful for the doctor's help. "I mean," she said slowly, "that in my whole life nothing has ever happened to me."

Again the sound of her own voice, so calm and controlled, surprised her. She looked up at Dr. Nyquist, but her expression had not changed. The doctor pressed her fingertips together in front of her face in a gesture that reminded Mary Alice fleetingly of her father about to offer up a prayer. She said nothing for a moment. She seemed to be thinking.

Then she said quietly, "But something did happen that brought you here."

Mary Alice nodded. "Yes," she said.

"You made something happen."

Mary Alice looked down at the bedspread. She felt it coming back, the feeling of tightness, confusion, tying her up inside. The doctor was edging close to something, something that frightened her.

The doctor retreated.

"No," she said, lowering her hands to her lap. "I don't think you are ready yet to talk about it. Instead let us try something else. I would like you to get as comfortable as possible. Now close your eyes and relax your whole body. Just rest that way for a moment."

Mary Alice closed her eyes. After a minute the turmoil subsided. Her body began to feel heavy, inert.

"Now I would like you to think back," said Dr. Nyquist's voice, "as far into the past as you can. I want you to try to find for me your earliest memory."

Mary Alice felt her thoughts floating away from her. Her mind emptied out; it was hollow like her body.

"The very first thing you can remember," came the doctor's voice again.

Mary Alice seemed to be sinking into empty space. It was like the half-sleep of her first days in the hospital. She felt removed from the room, yet safe, connected to reality by a thin thread.

A glimpse of something drifted into her consciousness, then drifted out again. She pulled at it, trying to get it back, put it into focus. She saw it again. A girl in a yellow dress and patent leather shoes sitting on a church bench.

She was three years old or maybe four, and she sat with her mother in the very last pew, near the door in case she or her brother had to be taken out during the service. Peter sat on her mother's other side, and her mother took turns drawing pictures for them on a little pad of paper to keep them quiet. Every few minutes Peter would whisper or wriggle in his seat—he never could sit still— and her mother would frown warningly at him. But Mary Alice always sat perfectly still, her feet straight out in front of her, the world reflected in her patent leather shoes. She was happy to be there, pressed close to the warmth of her mother, looking up at her father in the front of the church.

He stood behind a carved wooden pulpit high up on a platform. In his flowing black robe he looked bigger than she knew him to be, like a giant or a king. And he seemed to possess a physical power that he did not display at other times. His arms waved in the air and his eyes flashed; his face was intense with feeling. And he spoke in a different voice. It soared high and rumbled low, it implored and chastised, it was full of joy and of anger. He was a different being than the man she knew as her father.

And he talked of strange things. She could not follow most of what he said and did not try, as with most adult conversations. But some words she noticed because they

were repeated again and again. Savior. Sin. Righteous-
ness. Judgment Day. Father. Son. Holy Ghost.

"In the name of the Father and the Son and the Holy
Ghost. Amen." Those were the words he always used at
the end of the prayer. She knew it was the prayer because he folded his hands and closed his eyes like he did
at home before the start of a meal, and her mother did
too. After awhile—she didn't know how long—she came
to understand that the Father was God and the Son was
Jesus. God looked something like Santa Claus, very old
with a long white beard, kind-looking, but also a little
bit scary. He lived in a place called Heaven somewhere
up in the sky, and you couldn't see him. Jesus was his
son, and he had been a real man with long brown hair
and a white robe and gentle eyes. He had walked all over
teaching people how to be good, but then some bad
people had put him on a cross and he died and went to
Heaven too. Now he and God were there together, and
the two of them ran the world. But Mary Alice never
could figure out who the Holy Ghost was. For awhile she
thought it might have something to do with Halloween,
but that didn't seem to make sense. Her father never explained it and Mary Alice didn't ask. She seldom asked
questions. Then it gradually came to her who the Holy
Ghost was. The Holy Ghost was her father.

Mary Alice opened her eyes.

"Have you remembered something?" asked Dr. Nyquist.

Mary Alice nodded. Slowly, hesitantly, she began to

tell the doctor about her first view of her father. Dr. Nyquist listened carefully, saying little. When Mary Alice was finished, she asked, "How long did you go on thinking that your father was the Holy Ghost?"

Mary Alice frowned, trying to remember. "I think I was about six or seven when I said something to Peter about it. And he laughed."

That laugh came back to her now. Not scornful or mean—Peter was never mean—but incredulous. "What? You mean you think that the Holy Ghost is our father? Oh, Mary Alice." He had explained to her then that the Holy Ghost was some sort of spirit—she didn't understand what that meant—and that even though their father was a minister of God, he was just an ordinary man.

"And did you believe that? Did you believe that your father was an ordinary man?"

Mary Alice thought back to that conversation, her brother's face so serious, her own hot with embarrassment. Shame at having her brother, who was always so smart, think that she was dumb. She remembered nodding vigorously, assuring Peter that she understood.

"No," she said now. "I didn't believe it. Not really."

"Why?"

"There was something—something different about my father. He wasn't like other people." Mary Alice's voice trailed off as her thought ran down.

"Can you remember what it was that made him not like other people?"

Mary Alice felt as if she were back again sitting on the

hard church bench, looking up at that tall robed figure in the front of the church. "He was always somehow—apart from things. Even when he wasn't wearing his robe and standing up in church. At home he didn't do the ordinary kinds of things that other people's fathers did, like fixing things around the house or going shopping or playing ball in the back yard. He was always in his study. Or if he did do those things once in a while, it seemed like he wasn't really there, his mind was somewhere else. As if he was too—I don't know—too good to be part of it."

"Too good?" repeated the doctor.

Mary Alice nodded. "He was—he is—a completely good person. He has lived his whole life according to the teachings of the Bible. It is like an obsession with him. I don't think he ever told a lie or cheated on a test or anything like that in his whole life. If he came home and found that someone had given him too much change in a store—even if it was just a couple of pennies—he would get right back in the car and return it. That's the way he is—just good. And somehow when he looks at you, you get the feeling that he knows about you, that he can look inside your head and see the bad thoughts there."

The doctor was silent for a moment. Then she said, "This goodness of his that sets him apart, do you think that others feel it too, that it might make them uncomfortable?"

Mary Alice thought of her father, standing at the back of the church after the service was over, shaking hands with people. Even then he did not smile, she remembered.

He seemed remote, almost ill at ease, as if he had used up his capacity to reach out to them while standing in the pulpit and now his mind was somewhere else. It was her mother who talked to everyone, her mother standing a little apart from her father, her mouth frozen in a perpetual smile, asking people how they were, saying Yes, she'd be glad to bring a Swedish-meatball casserole to the covered-dish supper on Wednesday night, while Mary Alice stood there, her hand clutching her mother's skirt so she wouldn't lose her in the crush of coats and raised voices and clashing perfumes, waiting and waiting to go home.

"I think maybe he does make people uncomfortable," said Mary Alice. "Because he is not comfortable with them." She turned this new thought over in her mind, looking at it from all sides. It was true, she felt. Her father was not comfortable with the part of being a minister that meant going to meetings all the time and visiting sick people and calling on new families in town to see if they would like to join the church. He felt easy with books, the heavy old volumes in his study, the small worn Bible he always carried in his coat pocket, not with people. But there was more to it than that. Although he was not at ease with people, he seemed to have a need to serve them, to help them find God in the way that he himself had. It was more than a need: It was a commitment, a mission.

Another new thought came to Mary Alice. "Maybe that had something to do with why we moved so many times," she said. "He always seemed to be looking for something. I don't know what."

"Tell me about moving so many times," said Dr. Nyquist.

Mary Alice remembered the first church best. It was large, a great white building with carved wooden doors on the corner of a busy street. And inside, in the room where the services were held, everything was dark wood and soaring space, vast, overwhelming. Sitting in the last pew with her mother and Peter, she had to crane her neck to see the wooden chandeliers, eight of them, with lightbulbs shaped like candles that hung from the ceiling high above, the round stained-glass window in front with colors of the deepest reds and blues, the bronze organ pipes on the wall. The pulpit where her father stood seemed very far away; a microphone was needed to make his voice heard. And after the service was over and all the people had finally gone, the church echoed with Mary Alice's and Peter's footsteps as they walked along the rows of seats picking up the church bulletins that people had left behind.

When their father and mother were finally ready to leave, locking up the church behind them, they only had to go next door to their house, big and white like the church, with a tall Christmas tree growing in the front yard and swings in the back. She could remember every room in that house: the living room with its brick fire-place and blue rug, the bright yellow kitchen with the table next to the window where she and Peter would look for squirrels while they ate breakfast, the upstairs back porch where Peter liked to sleep on hot nights in the summertime, her bedroom with the pink curtains and bedspread that her mother made, the upstairs bathroom with the tub and the downstairs bathroom with no tub, the basement playroom. It had seemed to her a wonderful house, and she thought they would live there forever. She remembered the feeling of disbelief when her father had told them they were leaving it. She was five then, just finishing kindergarten. Her father drove them to the new house where they were going to live, in a nearby town, and she cried when she saw it. There was no Christmas tree and no swings, and it was ugly brown and looked dark inside. Her mother had seemed disappointed too, she recalled, but she told Mary Alice to stop crying, that a minister's family had to live in the house that the church gave them, and she would like it when they got their furniture inside, she would see.

But she never did. Even after her mother made new curtains for her bedroom, it still seemed dark and cramped. And the new church was smaller, and not so many people came to the services, and her father sang in the choir besides preaching because they only had four men singers. And the furnace kept breaking down. Her father was on the phone all the time, talking about getting money for a new furnace. For the first time Mary Alice became aware that money was something that concerned her father and mother and that for some reason they did not have as much of it as other people. When Mary Alice asked for something in a store, they almost always said it cost too much and she would have to wait for the school sale or the rummage sale or her mother would make it on her sewing machine. She didn't remember much more about living there—they were only at that church for three years—except that while they were in that house her sister was born.

She woke up one morning and was startled to find that her mother had gone to the hospital during the night and that she had a new sister named Julia. And Mrs. Ramsey was in the kitchen making breakfast. Mrs. Ramsey with white hair who did everything at the church, even typing up the Sunday bulletins, but who never smiled and wouldn't let Mary Alice and Peter do anything. She stayed with them for three days, only going home after supper each night, and then finally their mother came home with the new baby. Mary Alice remembered sitting on the front steps waiting for her father to bring them home. She and Peter were dressed up in their good clothes for some reason, and Mrs. Ramsey kept calling out the window to Peter to get back on the steps so he wouldn't get his shoes muddy. Mary Alice sat very still, her eyes focused on the end of the street so she would be sure to see their blue car the moment it turned the corner. And at last it came, rolling slowly down the street and into the driveway, and her mother got out, smiling, holding something wrapped up in a yellow blanket. Mary Alice didn't look at it, this foreign object that was supposed to be her sister. She was too busy staring at her mother. "Mommy," she said in amazement, "you're skinny again."

A few months later they moved again, this time to another state. It was very different there; the town was not surrounded by other towns but by farms and empty country, and there was a lot more snow in the winter. Mary Alice liked the snow, but that was all she liked about the new town. She couldn't walk to school, she had to ride in a school bus. And she and Peter went to different schools, so for a long time she sat all by herself in the front seat of the bus listening to the other children laughing and talking behind her. The church was much like the one they had just left, only smaller still, and her father worked harder than before. Not only did he sing in the choir but he taught Sunday school too, and for a while when the sexton left and they couldn't find another one, he even swept the floors of the church at night. Her mother said he shouldn't do it, it wasn't proper for a man in his position and he was letting the people in the church take advantage of him, but he did it anyway. The church people were different here. They talked differently and they dressed differently, and even though they didn't put much money in the collection plate on Sundays, they were always sending over homemade pies and boxes of fresh eggs and baskets of corn. And they listened very carefully and kept nodding their heads when her father preached about sin. It was something he talked about more and more, Mary Alice noticed. She was almost nine now and could understand most of what he said in his sermons. Sin and God's wrath and the Judgment Day: those were the words he repeated over and over. The forces of evil had grown strong in the world, he would warn, his voice full of gloom and despair. But the Day of Judgment would come, and when it did, he proclaimed, his voice rising, those who did not repent their sins would feel the fury of God's anger. They would burn forever in the fiery pits of Hell. (Mary Alice always shivered when he spoke of the fiery pits and resolved to repent, though she wasn't quite sure what it meant.) Her father seemed convinced that the Judgment Day was not far off. Yet in some ways he seemed happier than before. The new town reminded him of the town where he had grown up in Minnesota, he said. He talked more easily with people after church, asking them how they thought the rain would affect the corn crop and things like that. And on Sunday afternoons he liked to take long rides in the country, pointing out to Mary Alice and Peter what crops were growing and what kind of cows were grazing in the fields they passed. They stayed there for five years, long enough for Peter to graduate from high school, and Mary Alice to find a friend, and Julia to stop being a baby. And then, just when the church finally seemed to be gaining strength, so that her father no longer had to sing in the choir and there was talk of building an addition to make room for more Sunday school classes, her father said one night at dinner, "I have been called to another church."

And so they had come to West Greenville. A tiny church in a tiny town, a town that was struggling just to survive since the glove factory that had provided all the jobs had shut down. Her father had to start all over with a rundown church building that needed a new roof before winter and a congregation that seemed to argue among themselves about everything. And the strange thing was that her father seemed even happier. He closed himself up for hours in his little study in the attic and came out talking about the power of prayer and how God was going to provide the church with a new roof. And then, a few days later, Henry Pinkerton managed to get a load of shingles at wholesale prices, and her father and a few other men climbed up and worked for three days nailing them down themselves, and her father came home, his eyes bright with excitement, saying that a miracle had happened, praise the Lord.

Mary Alice couldn't figure it out. What drove her father to keep moving from church to church? When he moved, why wasn't he moving up to a better job like other people's fathers? Why couldn't he be satisfied with a comfortable job, a comfortable church? Why did he seem to look for problems?

Dr. Nyquist did not respond right away after Mary Alice had finished speaking. She sat with her legs crossed, looking past Mary Alice toward the window. She seemed to be studying the curtains.

Then she shifted in her chair, her eyes meeting Mary

Alice's in her direct, open way. "You said that your father always seemed to be looking for something," she said. "Do you think it might be that what he was looking for was his own beliefs? Sometimes it can take a long time to find out exactly who we are and where we fit into the world. And perhaps too he may have been searching for a place where he could feel needed, where he could make a difference."

Mary Alice nodded. She had never thought of it quite that way.

"But what concerns you and me is how this searching of your father's has affected his family. And you in particular. How did you feel about moving so many times?"

Mary Alice thought about it. About watching the moving men take away her white dresser and her rocking chair and her bed one by one until suddenly her room was not her room anymore. About driving down the streets of a new town for the first time, trying to find a store that was open to buy a quart of milk for breakfast. About walking next to her mother on legs grown suddenly shaky up the steps to a new school.

"Scared," she said, her voice almost a whisper.

Dr. Nyquist was silent for a minute.

"Were you upset with your father for making you move?"

Mary Alice hesitated. "I don't know. I—I don't think so. He was always so positive that he was doing the right thing. He would pray about it for days, locked up in his study, and then he would come out and tell us that God had spoken to him and told him it was His will. So it was not for us to question God's will."

"I see," said the doctor.

Mary Alice closed her eyes. In her mind she could see her father again as she had when she was three or four and sat with her mother in the last row at church. Up high on a platform, out of reach, yet dominating the room with his presence. His face stern, his hands outstretched, reaching upward. Speaking of things she did not understand in a voice she did not recognize.

She heard Dr. Nyquist say quietly, almost as if she were thinking out loud, "A righteous man, your father. To me he sounds a little bit like the Holy Ghost."

8

Russell Snow his name was. He had lived next door to them in the first house. He had dark hair and was small for his age; when he first moved in, before she knew his name, she called him "that tiny boy." He was her first friend.

They became best friends. They played together every day in her backyard or his. They rode their tricycles up and down the sidewalk. She let him play with her real-china dish set that her grandmother had sent her for her birthday. He took her dolls for rides in the red wagon he had gotten for his birthday.

One day they were in his backyard. Two of the dolls had fallen out of the wagon and had to be taken to the hospital. The hospital was behind the garage. Mary Alice laid the dolls down carefully in beds made of leaves and told them it was all right, Mommy was there and the doctor was coming to take care of them. Russell checked each of them to see if they had any broken arms or legs and bandaged the head of the baby doll, the one she called Betsy. Then he started to take their temperatures with a stick.

"All they have is a hole," he said.

"That's what girls have," said Mary Alice.

"You mean that's all you have?" asked Russell.

"Yes," said Mary Alice.

"I don't believe it," said Russell. "Show me."

Mary Alice hesitated. She didn't know why, but she thought she shouldn't.

"I'll show you mine," said Russell.

It was almost dinnertime. It was getting dark behind the garage, too dark to see clearly what they were showing each other. She remembered the stark outline of tree branches against the dull November sky. She remembered the rustle of dry leaves, ankle-deep around their feet. And the sudden awareness of someone else standing there with a strange expression on her face. Russell's mother.

She didn't say anything. She just picked up Mary

Alice's dolls and handed them to her and then walked with her to her house and rang the front doorbell. Mary Alice's mother opened the door. Mary Alice went in and started taking off her coat, and she could hear Russell's mother speaking to her mother in low tones that she couldn't understand. Then her mother looked at Mary Alice with that same strange expression, but she didn't say anything either. Nobody said anything until after dinner.

Mary Alice was in her pajamas in bed hugging her teddy bear tight because even though nobody had said anything she could feel that something was wrong. Her father came in as he always did to say good night. This was his best time of day, the time when he seemed most at peace. He sat on her bed and said her prayers with her, and sometimes he told her a little story from the Bible or something that had happened when he was a boy and used to visit his uncle's farm in the summer. Then he would kiss her forehead and turn out the light. But this time after her prayers were finished he remained sitting on the bed, not saying anything, just looking at her. In his eyes she could read something that he was trying to hide: anger. She squeezed her bear tighter.

"Mary Alice," he said finally, the anger concealed in a too-quiet voice, "I was very disappointed to hear what happened today. That was a bad thing—a sinful thing— for a little girl to do. You are never ever to do anything like that again. Your mother and Russell's mother have talked about your punishment, and they have agreed that you and Russell are not to play together for a week. Do you understand?"

Mary Alice understood that she had been right in thinking that there was something about that part of her body that was bad, that had to be kept secret, but she did not understand why. She did not ask, though, she only nodded, relieved that it was over. Her father seemed relieved too. His eyes softened somewhat and he leaned over and kissed her forehead as he always did and then turned out the light.

For the next few days she did not see Russell except out the window, getting into the car with his mother or riding his tricycle in front of his house or playing alone in his backyard. Once when her mother was in the basement doing the laundry Mary Alice saw him there, and she went outside. He looked up and saw her, but he did not wave or speak. For a few minutes they stood there, not looking at each other, and then she went inside again.

When the week of punishment was up, they went back to playing together. But something was not the same. Their talk did not flow as easily as before, and they avoided playing behind the garage. And then, soon after that, Mary Alice's father announced that they were moving. He said it was because God had called him to do His work in another church, but Mary Alice thought she knew the real reason. It was part of her punishment.

9

"Part of your punishment," repeated the doctor when Mary Alice told her. "Let's talk a little more about this. Were you punished often? Who did the punishing, your mother or your father?"

Thinking back, Mary Alice found that she could not remember very much about it. She could only see herself lying on the bed clutching her bear, her nose stuffed up from crying, waiting to hear her father's footsteps on the stairs coming to tell her she could come down now if she said she was sorry.

"I think it was mostly my father who punished us," she said. "It seemed as if it happened a lot. He was very strict. We would be punished for things like telling a lie or not doing what we were told or talking back. Peter was always being punished for that, but when he got older, he stopped arguing. He would just go to his room and read his science books. And we were punished for hitting each other and teasing Julia. And using bad language—my father thought even words like 'gosh' and 'gee whiz' were taking the name of the Lord in vain."

"And what was your punishment usually?"

"We had to go to our rooms and think about what we had done. And then after awhile my father would come upstairs and talk about why what we had done was bad."

"How did you feel about those talks?"

Mary Alice remembered exactly how she had felt lying face down on her bed, hearing her father's footsteps on the stairs. Relief mixed with dread and an awful helplessness. Faced with her father's anger, she knew she would never have the courage to say anything, to try to explain.

"They were—terrible. He would go on and on about how I had sinned against God and broken one of His Commandments and that kind of thing. He quoted the Bible a lot. He—he always had all the answers. I never felt there was anything I could say. And then, when the talk was over, he would make me go downstairs and apologize."

"Did he ever punish you physically—spank you, for example?"

"No. Never. He didn't believe in it."

Her father didn't even raise his voice when he was angry. That was the danger signal, when his voice grew very quiet. That and his eyes and the tightness in his jaw. Only once could Mary Alice remember seeing him come close to losing control. When Peter was about twelve, he had announced at the dinner table one night that God hadn't really created people the way it said in the Bible, that we had just come from a bunch of monkeys. Mary Alice remembered the look on her father's face: disbelief turning to anger, then to a silent rage. His eyes hardened; his usually pale face turned red. He stood up and took a step toward Peter, his hand raised. Mary Alice felt all of her muscles tense. Her stomach turned over. Was her father going to hit Peter? The thought of it—the sight of anger so open and intense—made her feel physically sick. She thought she would have to run from the room. But then her father stopped, his hand still in the air. For a moment the two of them stared at each other, and then, slowly, Mary Alice's father lowered his hand. Mary Alice saw that it was trembling. "Go to your room," he said to Peter, his voice deadly quiet. And Peter had gone.

"In a way it might have been better if he had spanked us," said Mary Alice. She hesitated, not quite sure of the rest of her thought. "Then it might have been—over with. Forgotten."

Dr. Nyquist nodded, as if in agreement. "But I get the

impression that neither of your parents were demonstra-
tive in a physical way, either in anger or affection."

It was true, Mary Alice thought. Her parents didn't
spank her, but they didn't hug her either. They rarely
showed affection outwardly, either to their children or to
each other. They seemed uncomfortable about things like
that. Did they feel it inside, though? She felt a sudden
pain so deep within her that it felt as if it were inside her
bones.

The doctor said nothing more. She sat with her chin
resting on her fingertips in what Mary Alice had come to
think of as her praying position. She wondered if the
doctor was aware of the reminder it gave of her father,
if she did it on purpose.

After a minute Dr. Nyquist asked, "Do you remember
any time as a child when you were not punished? When
you did something that you knew was wrong, but no one
found out about it?"

Mary Alice thought about it for a minute. Then she
nodded.

She stood in her pajamas at the bathroom sink. She was
about eight. She had been sick with an earache. Her
mother was pouring out the medicine from the jar into a
little plastic glass for her to swallow. After she drank it,
she was allowed to have some water because the medicine
had a bad taste (even though it was pink). Just then the
baby cried, and her mother had to go see what was wrong
with her.

Mary Alice was alone with the glass of awful-tasting

medicine. She remembered standing there for a long time, looking at it, smelling it, slowly raising it to her mouth. And then, as if directed by some unseen force, calmly pouring it down the sink.

"When my mother came back, she assumed that I had drunk it. She even said I was brave to drink it down so fast without complaining."

"And how did you feel when she said that?"

"Awful. All that day I kept thinking I was getting sicker. I even thought—I imagined that God was going to make me die as punishment." Mary Alice looked up to see Dr. Nyquist's reaction. The doctor did not smile. "At bedtime I was going to tell my father about it. I really wanted to tell him. But when it came time, I couldn't get the words out. I was afraid of what he would say, the way he would look at me. For a long time afterward I would think about that moment in the bathroom, and I would imagine that I really did swallow the medicine like my mother thought I did. After awhile I could see it so clearly in my mind that I almost convinced myself that I hadn't poured it down the sink after all."

"Almost," said the doctor softly. "But not quite."

She tapped her fingers together thoughtfully for a moment. Then she said, looking intently at Mary Alice, "And so you were punished after all. Wouldn't you say so?"

"I—yes, I guess so," said Mary Alice.

"By yourself. And that is the worst kind of punishment —the kind we give ourselves."

10

It was a sin, she knew, to want new things. For didn't the Bible say, "Lay not up for yourselves treasures on earth, where moth and rust doth corrupt, and where thieves break through and steal. But lay up for yourselves treasures in heaven"? Her father was always quoting that verse in his sermons to show that money was the root of all the evil in the world.

And that was how he lived. He didn't care what he

wore. He would wear shirts until the collars were so frayed that her mother couldn't mend them anymore. He wore the same suit every Sunday, dark blue with a very narrow gray stripe, the same suit every Sunday for seven or eight years until her mother finally convinced him that it was worn out, and then he went out and bought another one just like it at the factory-outlet store. The living room furniture was the same couch and two chairs that he and her mother had bought when they were first married, covered with slipcovers that her mother made every few years. They didn't have a dishwasher or a clothes dryer or a lot of other appliances that other people had. They didn't even have a TV set until someone in the church finally gave them an old black-and-white one when Mary Alice was in the fifth grade. Her father said they couldn't afford it and besides, there was nothing on TV worth watching, it was all sin and violence. He believed that the Lord would provide what was needed to sustain them, and the Lord did.

Only what the Lord provided, it seemed to Mary Alice, was mostly secondhand. All the cars they ever had were four or five or six years old when they got them. Mary Alice's father always believed their owners when they said they were as good as new, but once he had bought them, it seemed as if something was always going wrong with them. Most of Peter's and Mary Alice's and Julia's clothes, except the ones that Mary Alice's mother made herself, came from rummage sales or school sales or sometimes from church people whose own children had outgrown them. For a while Mary Alice was dressed almost entirely in clothes that used to belong to a girl named Elsie Pettingill. Elsie's mother kept on sending over shopping bags full of skirts and blouses, dresses and dress-up coats. "Just look at these, they've hardly even been worn," Mary Alice's mother would say. "And they're from all the best stores. Wasn't that nice of Mrs. Pettingill to think of you?" Mary Alice couldn't bring herself to say that she thought both Elsie and all of Elsie's clothes were ugly. "They smell funny," she finally said one time, and her mother replied briskly, "Why, it's just a little mildew. I'll put them through the machine a couple of times and they'll be as good as new."

A lot of their toys came from rummage sales too and somehow were never quite what Mary Alice had had in mind, or else they had a part missing so they didn't do what they were supposed to do. Peter's bicycle was second-hand, bought from a neighbor down the street. When Mary Alice was old enough for a two-wheeler too, she asked for one for Christmas. She described very carefully in her letter to Santa Claus exactly the kind she wanted: red and white with a basket and a shiny silver bell, just like her friend Joyce's. When she came downstairs on Christmas morning, she was disappointed not to find it under the tree. But then, after all the presents had been opened, her mother said, "You know, it seems to me that I saw something out in the garage. Maybe it was a present that Santa Claus couldn't fit down the chimney. Mary Alice, why don't you go and look?" And Mary Alice ran out to the garage, and there in the corner with a green ribbon tied on its handlebars was a bicycle. Only it wasn't red and white, and it didn't have a basket, and the bell was so rusty that it wouldn't ring. It was a secondhand bike—even worse than that, a boy's bike. Mary Alice had tried to act happy, to feel happy, because at least it was a bike to ride. But she felt leaden inside and could hardly force herself to say, "It's very nice. Thank you." Later Peter had whispered to her, "I'll help you paint it. It'll look great, you'll see." And they did paint it, red with white racing stripes on the fenders, which made it a little better but still couldn't conceal the fact that it was an old bike, a boy's bike.

One day not long after that—it was still Christmas vacation—Mary Alice's mother took her and Peter shopping at the five-and-ten. They had to buy Peter some notebooks and pencils for school, and her mother said Mary Alice could pick out some barrettes to go with the new Sunday-school dress she was making her.

Mary Alice went right to the hair counter, while her mother and Peter went to the back of the store to look at notebooks. It always took Peter forever to make up his mind. He had to check every single notebook to see which had the most pages and which had the kind of lines he liked, and weigh all sorts of other considerations. Mary Alice didn't like standing around waiting while he did it.

She saw the barrettes she wanted right away. They were green and white and shaped like bows, her favorite kind.

She slid the card off the hook and, with it in her hand, wandered over to the next counter, which was jewelry.

Mary Alice loved to look at jewelry. She loved the bright colors, the flower shapes, the shiny chains of gold and silver. If she had to choose just one of the necklaces it would be almost impossible, they were all so pretty. Of course she couldn't choose one; her mother had said "No, it's a waste of money" so many times that Mary Alice had stopped asking. It wasn't just the money even. Her father didn't approve of jewelry or fancy clothes. God created us the way we are, he believed, and it was wrong to want to change His handiwork. There was a verse in the Bible about that too, which he sometimes quoted. It had something to do with lilies in a field.

But Mary Alice could look. She picked out a gold chain with little yellow daisies and put it on. Then she found another she liked—red and blue beads alternating with white ones. And another—bright orange beads shaped like eggs of all different sizes. She stood on her tiptoes to see how she looked. Then she noticed something else next to the mirror. A blue velvet card full of rings.

They were all gold. Some were shaped like flowers, with yellow or white or blue petals, and some like butterflies. And some had stones, round or square. There was one with a pink stone near the bottom of the card. Pink, her favorite color.

Mary Alice reached up and took it off the card. She held it in her hand, turning it to catch the light. The stone was the palest shade of pink, a smoky hazy color, with tiny flecks of green hidden deep inside. When the light struck it, the ring sparkled like a fabulous jewel. It was beautiful.

Carefully Mary Alice slipped the ring onto the middle finger of her right hand. Surprisingly, it was not too big. It fit perfectly.

She stood there looking at the ring on her finger. It looked right, felt right, as if it had always been part of her. She thought that the ring had been waiting here for her, waiting to give her its shining beauty.

"Mary Alice, we're ready to go. Did you find your barrettes?"

Her mother and Peter were coming toward her down the aisle, each carrying a brown paper bag.

Without thinking about it Mary Alice put her right hand into the pocket of her bluejeans. All by itself the ring seemed to slip from her finger. It nestled into the folds of the pocket, tucked away, gone, yet reassuringly near.

"These barrettes will be fine with your dress, Mary Alice. Now take off all those necklaces, and let's try to find a saleslady. We're late. I told your father we'd be home by five to start dinner."

One by one Mary Alice took off the necklaces and put them back on the counter. She followed her mother to the cash register on the next aisle where she was paying for the barrettes. And then to the car.

All the way home, sitting in the back seat, Mary Alice could feel the presence of the ring. It was there, a tiny bump next to her leg, warm, almost like a live thing. She felt possessed of a marvelous secret and she smiled, looking out the window at the passing cars.

But when she got home, upstairs in her room with the door closed, and took the ring from her pocket, she was suddenly filled with horror. What was she doing with this ring? Where had it come from? It was not hers. How had it gotten into her pocket?

She looked at it, winking in the palm of her hand. There was something hard, almost sinister, about its beauty now.

And then she heard footsteps on the stairs. Her father's footsteps. Mary Alice's heart pounded wildly. She had to hide the ring before her father saw it. He would know immediately that she had done a terrible thing. That she had sinned.

Hurriedly she opened the top drawer of her dresser and thrust the ring inside, into a pile of her underpants. Then she snatched up the book that was on her night table, opened it somewhere in the middle, and sat down on the bed.

There was a knock on the door.

"Time for dinner, Mary Alice," said her father's voice.

Her mouth was dry, too dry to speak. But she had to answer.

"Coming," she managed to say hoarsely.

There was silence outside the door. Then she heard her father moving on down the hall to the bathroom. He was not coming in. She was safe.

But she knew she was not really safe as long as she had the ring. She couldn't keep it in the dresser drawer. Her mother was always opening her drawers, putting in clean clothes, arranging everything in neat little piles. She noticed when anything was different. There was no hiding place in her room—in the whole house—that would be safe from her mother. Her mother saw everything.

She would take the ring back to the store. Take it back and put it up on the blue velvet card when no one was looking, and it would be as if nothing had ever happened. Only she couldn't figure out how to get back to the store. The five-and-ten was in a shopping center in the next town. It was too far to walk or ride her bike and she couldn't ask her mother to drive her.

She would mail it back. That was the thing to do. Put it in an envelope and mail it to the store. But then she would have to write the store's name and address on the envelope. And stores had detectives who looked at the handwriting and could figure out who had written it, and then they came and arrested that person. No, she couldn't mail it back.

She would have to get rid of the ring. She thought about flushing it down the toilet. But what if it wouldn't go down? What if it clogged up the pipes and her mother had to call the plumber and he fished around inside with his wires and came up with the ring, holding it out to her mother, saying, "Here is the cause of your problem"?

She could sneak it into the garbage can, but then the same thing might happen. The garbage man would knock at the back door. "Pardon me," he would say to her mother, "but surely you didn't mean to throw away this valuable ring."

Finally she decided to bury it in the backyard. She chose a spot far away from her mother's flower garden, far from where she and Peter had buried their turtles that died, way in back near the fence. The ground was frozen and she had to work hard to make a hole with a sharp stick, hurrying to finish before someone came and saw what she was doing. At last she succeeded in digging a hole about two inches deep. She took off her mitten and turned it carefully upside down. The ring fell out in her hand. Without looking at it again she dropped it into the hole and covered it up with dirt.

That night she dreamed that a man with a bulldozer was in their backyard, digging it up to turn it into a garden. There were holes everywhere, and in the middle of them stood her father, directing the man, saying, "Over here. Now over here." The dream was so real that she woke up and went over to the window to see if it was true. But instead of holes she found the backyard covered with snow. She was safe.

Except that when the snow melted and spring came, she started worrying about what would happen if her mother decided to plant flowers back by the fence this year. Or if a squirrel remembered that it had buried an acorn at that spot. Or if the spring rains were so heavy that they washed away the dirt covering the ring. She hadn't buried it deep enough.

She didn't stop worrying until the day in May when she found out that they were moving again. And not really until a month later, when the moving men came and they were all packed up and ready to drive to their new home in a different state. Looking out the back window of the car at the brown house for the last time, Mary Alice didn't feel sad to be moving. She felt relieved.

She was finally safe.

11

"Good morning, Mary Alice."

Dr. Nyquist set down a brown leather briefcase next to the bedside table and took off her raincoat. There were large dark spots splashed across the tan material. Raindrops. Mary Alice glanced at the window and noticed for the first time the drops running down the glass.

"What a day," said the doctor, shaking her head. "This ought to really bring out the flowers."

Mary Alice stared at the briefcase. The doctor had never brought a briefcase before. She wondered what was inside. A lot of folders, probably, with people's names on them. The names of the doctor's other patients. And her name. She could see the label, neatly typed—the doctor's typing would be as precise as everything else about her—reading: *M. A. Fletcher.* She was a file number, a case.

Mary Alice decided not to tell the doctor about the ring after all.

Dr. Nyquist's eyes followed Mary Alice's eyes.

"Ah," she said softly, "the briefcase." She looked at it for a long moment. "It is a bit frightening, isn't it? So important-looking."

She lifted the briefcase onto her lap. "Now," she said, smiling, "I will share with you a little secret." One by one she unsnapped the brass latches, turning the case around so Mary Alice could see inside.

"This is what I carry in my important-looking brief-case," she said.

Inside was a sandwich wrapped in plastic, a Thermos bottle, a pad of yellow paper, and a little pile of three or four magazines—psychological journals, they appeared to be.

"I'm writing an article," explained the doctor, "and the only time I seem to get to work on it is during lunchtime in my office. Provided there are no interruptions. Mostly, I'm afraid, I just carry it back and forth."

She closed the briefcase, still smiling.

"Now," she said, "I wonder if you've thought of something you would like to talk about today."

Mary Alice found herself nodding. "Yes," she said. "I did."

But after she finished telling Dr. Nyquist about the ring, the doctor didn't say any of the things Mary Alice had thought she would say. Like how did you feel about that? Or something about being punished or not being punished. She just nodded and said, "That must have been very frightening." Then she looked past Mary Alice toward the window, as if she were checking on the weather. It was still raining, Mary Alice saw.

The doctor looked back at the bed. "I've been wondering," she said, "how it felt to be part of a minister's family. We have talked quite a bit about your father and his strong religious beliefs. But how did the other members of the family feel about the religion you were exposed to so constantly?"

Mary Alice turned the question over in her mind. She thought about the way it used to be when they were little, she and Peter dressed up in their Sunday clothes, going to Sunday school. She and Peter singing "Jesus Loves Me" and "Jesus Wants Me for a Sunbeam," listening raptly while the Sunday-school teacher read them the stories of Noah's ark and Joseph and his coat of many colors and Jesus feeding the multitudes with a few loaves of bread and some fishes, receiving gold stars for each Bible verse they recited. But then, later, things changed. Peter had grown up and started asking questions. It had begun, Mary Alice thought, with the time Peter had challenged his father about people being descended from monkeys. Instead of keeping quiet after that, Peter had kept on asking questions at the dinner table, as if oblivious to his father's reaction: How could anyone really know that there was a Heaven and Hell since no one had ever come back to tell about it? How could people believe every word of a book that had been written so many thousands of years ago? And how could her father be positive that God even existed? This last question upset her father so much—and Mary Alice too, watching him, her stomach churning so that she was unable to take another bite of her meat loaf—that after that Peter seemed more careful what he asked about. And when he was about fifteen, he stopped asking questions altogether. Not that he didn't still think about them, she was sure. But realizing how painful they were for his father, he kept them to himself. Peter the scientist. Mary Alice knew what he believed; he had told her once. "If you can see something or can prove that it exists, it exists. Otherwise it's just wishful thinking."

"I don't think Peter believes in God," Mary Alice said quietly. "At least he has a lot of doubts. And he doesn't believe in all the things my father is always talking about: Hell and the Judgment Day and everything. 'Hocus-pocus,' he calls all of that. Peter is too much of a scientist to accept it. But he doesn't talk about it with my parents anymore. He goes to church when he's home and listens and is polite. He just doesn't get involved."

And Julia? Julia was easy.

"My sister is just the opposite. She believes every word my father says, everything she's been taught in Sunday school. Of course, she's only nine. But I think that's just the way she is. She never has any doubts or asks any questions. She just accepts things. When she grows up, she will still believe everything she believes now."

"And you?" asked the doctor.

"I—I'm not sure," Mary Alice answered.

There was nothing about it that she felt sure of. Maybe Peter was right, maybe religion was all a lot of wishful thinking so that people wouldn't feel so scared about dying and turning into pieces of dust. Maybe there was no God, only biology. It didn't seem logical, any of it, from a scientific point of view. Could there really be such places as Heaven and Hell? If they existed, why hadn't anyone ever come across them when they went into outer space? And what about Jesus? Had he been a real person, or was it all just a story someone had made up? Could he really have healed sick people and risen from the dead and performed all the miracles her father always talked about? Or was it a hoax of some kind? She found it hard to believe in miracles, especially ones that had happened so long ago. There were always explanations, like the one she had read in the newspaper recently about the brightness in the sky at the time of Jesus' birth being due to some comet or something.

And yet there was something in her that believed, or wanted to believe, in God. She thought of Him still, as she had when she was little, as sitting somewhere up in the sky looking down on the earth, watching everything, knowing everything. He was kind of like a great scorekeeper. Only He knew things like how many squirrels lived in the woods behind her house, what was really out there in space beyond the stars, and whether she would ever get married and have children. She would find herself talking to Him sometimes, sending up little prayers. It was a habit from when she was little and said her prayers every night. But it was reassuring to think there was someone there—maybe even necessary. Otherwise, what was the point of anything?

"I don't know what I believe," Mary Alice said. "Not everything my father does. I can't believe in miracles—I don't think so anyway. It would be nice to believe in Heaven, to think that death isn't the end of everything, but I'm not sure. And Jesus—I think he existed and was a good man, but I don't know if he was really the Son of God. I don't know what to believe. But I would like to believe something."

Dr. Nyquist nodded. After a minute she said, "And your mother? What about her? Would you say she is as religious as your father?"

It seemed to Mary Alice a strange question. Her mother's whole life revolved around the church. She never missed a Sunday service. She never missed a meeting of any of the church organizations she belonged to. She was always knitting mittens for the Spring Fair or baking cookies for the Bake Sale or collecting old clothes for the church's Mission to Africa. She was just as involved with the church as Mary Alice's father. And yet there was something different about her involvement, something that Mary Alice couldn't quite put her finger on. What was it?

Thinking about it, it occurred to her that her father's involvement was on the inside, inside his head. Religion was what he thought about all the time. While her mother's involvement seemed more on the outside. She hurried around doing all these church things, but what was she really thinking about? What was in her mind when she closed her eyes in church? Was she praying, or was she deciding what kind of casserole to make for next week's Pot-luck Supper? Mary Alice didn't know. Her mother never talked about it. She didn't talk about religion, only about the church.

Mary Alice shook her head slowly. "I don't know," she said. "I think maybe—maybe she isn't."

"What makes you think that?"

"I'm not sure. She doesn't talk about it like my father does. She does all the things a minister's wife is supposed to do, but—I don't know. It seems like a ritual, like she's doing what is expected of her."

Was she being fair to her mother? Mary Alice wondered. Maybe her mother's faith was as strong as her father's, but she just didn't like to talk about it.

"Expected of her by whom?" asked the doctor. "The members of the church?"

Mary Alice nodded. "The church people, the town people. Everyone. That's what really is most important to her—what people think."

It seemed to Mary Alice that it was what her mother talked about most of the time. She could remember when she was very small and her mother would take her and Peter to a department store. They would get tired of standing there waiting and would start crawling under the racks of clothes, pretending they were hiding in a cave. "Come out of there this minute!" their mother would hiss, looking over her shoulder to see if any of the salesladies were watching, her face flushing bright pink. "Whatever will people think of you?" The same thing happened when they went to the doctor or dentist and had to sit in the waiting room. Or the few times they ate out in a restaurant. Mary Alice could remember the first time they ever went to a restaurant—it was on a Mother's Day, after church—and Peter dropped his pickle in his milk. Their mother got all upset. "I just knew we shouldn't have come," she said to their father. "They're too young to take to a restaurant. Now everyone is looking at us."

Mary Alice didn't think everyone was looking at them. Most of the people seemed to be looking at their dinners. But if anyone was looking at them, it was because their mother was making such a fuss.

"And look who's just come in," she went on. "The Allens. Wouldn't you know it? I'm sure they see us. You'd better wave to them, John. Children, sit up straight."

And then, miraculously, their mother's anxious face

broke into a beaming smile. "Why, hello there," she called. "So nice to see you."

Mary Alice's mother always thought everyone was watching them. That was because they were the minister's family. The minister's family had to behave; they had to set a good example. At church they couldn't whisper or run up and down the aisles after the service was over or hit anyone even if the other child hit first. They couldn't go back for seconds of dessert at church suppers. They couldn't do anything at all hardly, except breathe, on Sunday afternoons in case anybody might think they weren't observing the Sabbath. And later on, when they were older, there were places they couldn't go and certain kids they couldn't play with because it wouldn't look right for the minister's family.

When Mary Alice was about ten or eleven, she started having dreams. It was one dream really, but she kept having it over and over again. She dreamed she went to church with her mother—she didn't know where Peter and Julia were, but they weren't in the dream—and there was no one there. Her father was standing up front in the pulpit and the organist was playing, but there were no people in the church. Or sometimes just a very few people. And there she sat, she and her mother, in the middle of an empty pew singing the hymns all alone.

It was a frightening dream. It seemed to Mary Alice to mean that no one wanted to come to hear her father preach. And if no one came to hear him preach, he would have no church. And then what would happen to them?

Mary Alice got to be afraid that the dream would come true. The church they were at now was the smallest her father had had. Sometimes fewer than a hundred people came to the service on Sunday. Especially if it rained. Not as many people came to church when it rained. Mary Alice began to dread rainy Sunday mornings. So on rainy Sunday mornings she got sick.

Right after breakfast her stomach would start to hurt, and when it was almost time to get dressed for church, she would say to her mother, "I don't feel well." Her mother would take her temperature, though she never had any, and would ask, "Do you feel like you might throw up?" and Mary Alice would say Yes, and then her mother would say, "Well, maybe you'd better stay home." And Mary Alice would go to her room and lie down on her bed and read while everyone else went to church. And when they got home, she would be feeling better, well enough to have lunch.

After this happened a few times, Mary Alice's mother got worried and took her to the doctor. The doctor poked and pushed on her stomach and asked her a lot of questions and then told her mother he couldn't find anything wrong. After that her mother wouldn't let her stay home from church anymore.

"But it really does hurt," Mary Alice would say. And it was true. When she thought about it hurting, it really did.

"I'm sure it's just nerves," her mother answered. "But we'll sit near the door in case you need to run out to the bathroom."

"Oh, why don't you let her stay home?" Peter came into the kitchen, yawning, still in pajamas and bare feet. "What difference does it make if we aren't all in church every single Sunday?"

Mary Alice's mother looked shocked. "It makes a lot of difference," she said. "We are the minister's family. What would people think if the minister's own family didn't come to church?"

Dr. Nyquist didn't seem to find it surprising that her mother was this way. "It's natural for people in your parents' position to be somewhat concerned with what others think," she said. "Whether we think it's fair or not, people are more conscious of the behavior of, say, the principal's family or the mayor's family or the minister's family than they are of the rest of the community. It's too bad for you; it's a disadvantage of your father's profession. But you're saying that you feel your mother carries this concern to extremes, puts it before anything else?"

Mary Alice nodded slowly. It always surprised her how the doctor was able to put so precisely into words the thoughts that swirled around confusedly inside Mary Alice's head.

"Before her religion perhaps?"

For some reason Mary Alice felt suddenly afraid. It seemed to her that the doctor was sending her down a path she didn't want to take, one she had been trying to avoid.

She looked down at the bedspread. White, always white. Why did everything in a hospital have to be white? Why didn't they have bright colors, flowers, to cheer the patients up?

"It's all right," Dr. Nyquist said softly. "What we find out we will find out together."

What was she afraid of? Something about her mother. What was it about her mother that she did not want to know?

"My mother goes through the motions," Mary Alice said abruptly, still looking down, "but she doesn't mean it."

There was a pause, and then the doctor said, "You mean that you don't think she is sincere about her religion, that she doesn't practice it in her own life?"

Mary Alice nodded. That was it. She had taken the first step down the path.

"Can you think of an example for me?"

It was hard. Thinking of her mother now, she saw her smiling, always smiling, as she chatted with people after church. She always complimented them on their new clothes, always remembered to inquire about their illnesses, always thanked them five or six times for anything they had done for the church. She was so friendly, so nice.

And yet behind the smile she was different. On the way home in the car she would say to Mary Alice's father, "Did you see Marge Trumbull's hair this morning? I don't know how someone her age has the nerve to wear her hair like a teen-ager." Or "I just couldn't get away from Gladys Rivlin. And all she wants to talk about is her arthritis." Or "I understand that the Women's League is going to give us silver candlesticks for Christmas this year. Can you imagine? I'll never use them. I must have six sets of silver candlesticks already."

There was something in her voice, a sharpness, an edge, that didn't match her smile. It always made Mary Alice uneasy.

And then there was Mrs. Braxton.

Mrs. Braxton was the lady who lived next door to them. She was a tiny, white-haired lady, and she lived in a house that was almost as tiny as she was. Her husband had died a long time ago, and she had never had any children, so she lived by herself. Not really by herself, though, because she had five cats. "My children," she called them. She talked to them as if they were people, and she had even given them people's names. There was Arthur and Harry, who was the one who was always getting into trouble, and Sara and Emily, who were sisters, and the little one, whom she called Baby June. "She's my little sweetie, my little June bug," Mrs. Braxton would coo, giving Baby June a kiss on the nose, which Mary Alice thought was carrying things a little far.

Mrs. Braxton was a wonderful neighbor. She was always bringing over flowers from her garden or jam she had made, and she remembered everyone's birthday. She would take care of Julia anytime Mary Alice's mother wanted her to, and she wouldn't hear of being paid. It was the least she could do for the minister, she said. Julia loved to go to Mrs. Braxton's house. It was like having a grandmother right next door. Their one real grandmother who was still living was far away in Minnesota.

Then why was Mary Alice's mother so mean about the cats? She never missed a chance to say something bad about them, how they made Mrs. Braxton's house smell, how she'd read that they carried diseases, how disgusting it was to hear a grown woman talking baby talk to a dumb animal. And she didn't just say these things to Mary Alice's father or to her friends, she said them right in front of Mrs. Braxton too.

It was kind of in disguise, the things she'd say. Like "Now, Julia, don't forget to wash your hands after you play with the cats. I'm sure they're very clean, Mrs. Braxton, but they do roam all over, don't they? We don't really know where they've been." Or "That black cat of yours has been trying to get into the garbage cans again. What's his name? I can never keep track of their names, there are so many of them." Or "Ethel Sanders and Marge Trumbull are going down to Florida to visit the Nelsons next month. You should plan a trip like that sometime, Mrs. Braxton. But I don't suppose you'd leave the cats, would you?"

She was always smiling when she said these things, smiling as if to show there couldn't possibly be any harm intended, and Mrs. Braxton would smile too, as if to show she knew there was no harm intended. But Mary Alice wondered how she really felt inside.

One time Mary Alice's mother had gone even further. It was after the cats had knocked over three of Mrs. Braxton's prize African violets while she was out at a senior citizens' meeting at the church.

Mrs. Braxton was almost in tears.

"They're all ruined," she said. "And just when they were finally starting to bloom. That bad Harry. I know it must have been him."

Mary Alice's mother nodded sympathetically. "It's a shame," she said, "after all your work. That cat just seems to be naturally destructive."

"Well, you know he doesn't really mean to do it," Mrs. Braxton said. "It's just that he gets lonesome when I go out for so long."

"I wonder, Mrs. Braxton," Mary Alice's mother said. "Now I know it's none of my business, but have you ever thought of giving the cats away? You could do so much more with your gardening if you didn't have them to worry about, maybe even get one of those little green-houses they sell now. And you would be able to go out more, take a trip to Florida or out to Ohio to see your brother. I suppose it would be hard to find homes for so many cats, but you know, you could take them to the veterinarian and have them put to sleep."

This time Mary Alice could see, just for an instant, the flicker of hurt in Mrs. Braxton's eyes. "Oh, no," she murmured, "I could never do that." Then Mrs. Braxton turned away, buttoning her coat, putting on her gloves. "Well, I must be getting back. It's time to give the children their supper."

Mary Alice felt a prickling of something inside of her. She recognized it as anger. Why did her mother have to say that to Mrs. Braxton? Mary Alice opened her mouth to say something, something that would erase that look in Mrs. Braxton's eyes. And then she closed it again. She could never seem to express these feelings. She was frightened, somehow, that if she ever did, if ever she took the lid off of the angry feelings that bubbled inside her, they would boil over. There would be some kind of explosion. She had to keep them covered up.

But why had her mother said that? Why would she want to hurt anyone as nice as Mrs. Braxton? Didn't she understand that the cats were all the family Mrs. Braxton had, that whatever people might think of her talking to them and kissing them, she needed them? Couldn't her mother imagine how she might feel if she had no husband, no children? Why was Mary Alice able to put herself in Mrs. Braxton's place if her mother couldn't?

Mary Alice asked the doctor all these questions after she had told her the story.

Dr. Nyquist didn't answer right away. She always seemed to take her time, gathering together her thoughts, arranging them in order before putting them into words.

"Those are interesting questions," she said finally. "And difficult ones. I don't know why your mother would want to hurt Mrs. Braxton, consciously or unconsciously. But right now I am interested in what you are saying about how you see your mother. You seem to feel that she lacks compassion for others. Behind her smiling facade, she is not the warm caring person she appears to be—that you so much want her to be. She keeps herself at an emotional distance from people—from you. And this is difficult for you to accept."

Mary Alice nodded. She found suddenly that she was looking at the doctor through a blur of tears.

Dr. Nyquist went on, her voice very quiet. "It is hard to accept because we all want to feel that our mothers are close to us. And, if you allow yourself to believe that your mother is as removed from you in her way as your father is in his, then you are going to feel very much alone."

Mary Alice lay very still. She could hear the rain lightly splattering against the window. The tear in her left eye overflowed, and she felt it running very slowly down her cheek and into the corner of her mouth.

A scene flashed into her mind, a scene from long ago. She thought she had forgotten it. She and her friend Russell were on their tricycles. They had climbed the hill at the top of their street, which they weren't supposed to do because the hill was too steep to ride down. They sat there looking down, not sure what to do. Their houses seemed very far away. Mary Alice could just make out a dot of yellow on her door, which was the basket of flowers her mother had hung there because company was coming. And Russell's car parked in the driveway looked too small to ride in.

"I bet you're scared to go down," Russell said.

Mary Alice saw how the sidewalk seemed to dip and then straighten out and then dip again, and her stomach felt queasy. "I bet you are too," she said.

They sat there some more and then, without warning, Russell pushed off down the hill.

Mary Alice watched in astonishment. Russell passed the first dip safely. Now he was picking up speed, past the Fishbecks' house, past the Pilzers'. He had to take his feet off the pedals, he was going so fast. But still he was doing fine; it looked as though he was going to make it. He had passed the second dip and was almost to the Morriseys' house, where the sidewalk leveled off, when it happened. Maybe he hit a rock or something, but suddenly the tricycle swerved, seemed to balance for a moment on two wheels, and then tipped over.

For a long time nothing happened. Then Russell stood up. Mary Alice could see blood running down his arm onto his shorts, blood streaming from one knee. "Mommy!" he cried. And in another minute his mother was running out of the house, picking him up. She held him close, rocking him in her arms. And then they went inside.

Mary Alice sat on her bike looking down the hill. It was very quiet. No one seemed to be around. She wondered what to do. She thought she ought to walk her bike down the hill, after what had happened to Russell. But that took so long. And Russell had almost made it. Maybe she could do it. And if she didn't— A picture flashed through her mind of her mother running out to carry her into the house like Russell's mother had.

Without really deciding anything, just because she was tired of sitting there, Mary Alice lifted her feet a tiny bit off the sidewalk. The bike immediately rolled forward.

Mary Alice put both feet on the pedals to stop it. But it was too late. The bike was already going too fast. It had been scary watching Russell go down the hill, but doing it herself was terrifying. She didn't even see the houses go by; everything seemed blurred together. She gave up trying to keep her feet on the pedals, just held on to the handlebars as tight as she could. And then she was aware of Russell's red overturned bike right ahead of her, not quite off the sidewalk. She swerved to miss it but her front wheel hit something else. And she felt the sidewalk hit her.

When she stood up she saw that, like Russell, her elbow and her knee were bleeding. No, both knees were bleeding. It was worse than Russell. She started to cry. But her mother didn't come rushing out of the house. No one seemed to hear her.

Mary Alice stood in the middle of the sidewalk for a minute, and then she started walking toward her house. Hardly able to see where she was going because of the tears and her hair all in her eyes, she climbed the front steps and opened the screen door.

Her mother was in the dining room, arranging the silver tea things on the white lace tablecloth.

"Mommy," sobbed Mary Alice.

"Mary Alice!" Her mother set down the teapot. "Oh, my goodness. Are you all right? What happened?"

Mary Alice couldn't answer.

Her mother came hurrying toward her. Mary Alice lifted up her arms.

And then her mother stopped.

"Oh, my, just look at all that blood. I can't get it on my dress, Mary Alice. John, come quickly! Mary Alice has skinned her knees."

Her mother looked down at the floor.

"Oh, no!" Her eyes filled with horror. "It's dripped on the rug. And the Middletons are due here in ten minutes. Now what are we going to do?"

12

"Mary Alice," whispered a voice. "Are you awake?"

She had been asleep. The talks with Dr. Nyquist tired her out. She often slept after they were over, a good dreamless sleep that seemed to wash away the effects of what had been said, like a wave smoothing over footprints in the sand.

"Mary Alice," came the voice again, nearer, more urgent. It was a voice that could not be denied.

Mary Alice opened her eyes and was startled to find herself looking into her mother's face. She was leaning over the bed, unexpectedly close. Mary Alice could see a light sprinkling of freckles across her nose that she had never noticed before. And a few gray hairs mixed in with the dark ones that fell across her forehead. Had they been there before? Or had she, Mary Alice, caused them to appear? Mary Alice lowered her eyes, feeling confused, remorseful. At the same time her mother drew back with a little laugh.

"Oh, you are awake, dear. I'm sorry to disturb you. You looked so peaceful sleeping there. But I can only stay a few minutes—I'm going to be tied up all day working on the Spring Fair—and I've brought you some good news. Your father is just so busy that he couldn't come today. It's Easter week, you know."

Mary Alice's mother unsnapped her brown purse and drew out a long white envelope.

"This came for you in today's mail. I just had to open it—I knew you wouldn't mind. But I thought you would like to read it yourself."

She handed the envelope to Mary Alice.

Mary Alice stared at it blankly. *Miss Mary Alice Fletcher,* it said in fancy typewriter script. In the upper left-hand corner was a small embossed gold cross, encircled by the words *Bob Parker University.* And below that, *Office of the Dean of Admissions.*

Mary Alice did not want to open it.

"Come, Mary Alice. Please open it."

Mary Alice turned the envelope over and slowly drew out the letter inside.

Dear Mary Alice:

> I am most happy to inform you that your application for admission to Bob Parker University has been approved. This decision is the result of careful deliberation by the admissions staff and represents our confidence in you. We appreciate your interest in Bob Parker University and look forward to having you with us in September as a member of the freshman class.

There was more, about health history forms and room assignments and freshman orientation. Mary Alice could not read any more. But she kept her eyes on the piece of paper in her hand. She did not want to look up at her mother's face, to see the beaming, expectant smile she knew would be there.

"Well, dear, isn't that exciting news? Congratulations! We couldn't be more pleased. Your father is just thrilled. Bob Parker University is such a fine school. He thinks going there will be a wonderful experience for you."

Most happy to inform you . . . your application for admission to Bob Parker University has been approved. The words resounded inside Mary Alice's head.

"Mary Alice?"

Reluctantly Mary Alice raised her eyes. Her mother's smile had faded; a tiny frown creased her forehead.

"Aren't you pleased, dear?" she asked, her voice puzzled.

Marshaling all her resources, Mary Alice managed to nod her head.

Her mother's face brightened. "I know what's bothering you," she said. "You're concerned about finishing the year, having the credits to graduate. Well, you mustn't worry about that. I will speak to Mrs. Marwell—or maybe it would be better to talk with the principal. Anyway, I'm sure we can arrange something. As soon as you are feeling up to it, perhaps Katie can start bringing you some of your assignments. That way you won't get too far behind."

Mary Alice nodded again, feeling overwhelmed by her mother's energy, swept along by it as always.

For a moment their eyes met. Then her mother's darted away to the other side of the room.

"Those flowers are just about finished, I think. Why don't you ask the nurse to throw them out, and I'll bring you some fresh ones tomorrow. Our daffodils out back are just starting to bloom."

She stood up. "Well, I must be going. There is so much to do this week, I'm sure I don't know how it will all get done." She smiled down at Mary Alice. "Congratulations again, dear. Now that you have this to look forward to, I'm sure you'll get well very fast."

Leaning over, she brushed Mary Alice's cheek lightly with hers, her cheek that always surprised Mary Alice with its softness.

"Good-bye for now, dear."

And her mother was gone.

13

She was walking down a road with someone. It was a lady Mary Alice didn't know, but she was very nice. She kept smiling down at Mary Alice and stopping to pick flowers for her, and she held on to her hand so she wouldn't fall. Mary Alice was very little, and the lady's hand was soft and strong.

It was a beautiful sunny day. The road was somewhere in the country, and birds were singing. Mary Alice wasn't sure where they were or where they were going, but it didn't matter. She just wanted to keep on walking with this nice lady who was taking care of her.

They kept on walking, and after awhile Mary Alice noticed that it was starting to get dark. She said to the lady that maybe they ought to go home now, but the lady didn't seem to hear her. They kept walking down the road.

Now it was really getting dark. And the road was going through a deep forest. Strange shapes on either side leaned out to grab Mary Alice. She held on tighter to the lady's hand. She said again that she thought they should go home, but again the lady didn't answer. Mary Alice looked up at her, but it was so dark that she couldn't see her face anymore.

Suddenly Mary Alice was frightened. She wanted to go home right now. She tried to run, only she couldn't because the lady was holding her hand so tight. It didn't seem like the same soft hand she had held before. It didn't seem like the same nice lady who had been taking care of her.

And then somehow she was free of the hand and out of the woods, and running fast down the road toward home. The lady was somewhere behind, trying to catch her, but she couldn't because now Mary Alice was wearing roller skates and could go very fast. She went faster and faster, and she thought exultantly that the lady would never catch her. She was almost home.

But then the road changed. Without warning she came

to a steep hill, so steep that she couldn't see the bottom of it. And she couldn't stop. She was racing down the hill on her roller skates. It was so dark and so steep and she was going so fast.

She knew she was going to crash. She knew it, but she couldn't stop.

So dark. So steep. So fast.

14

"Well," said the doctor.

Mary Alice looked up. Dr. Nyquist was looking at her intently, a question in her eyes. Mary Alice wondered all at once if the doctor had soft cheeks, if the texture of her skin matched her voice and her smile. She would never know. The doctor was not her mother.

The smile was there again, gently prodding.

"Something has happened, I think, to upset you. Can you tell me about it?"

Mary Alice didn't see how the doctor could know. She had always been proud of the way she could conceal her thoughts from others. Like a spy, she used to think. A spy or a soldier. But the doctor seemed to know everything. Was it an ability she had acquired in becoming a psychologist? Or had she become a psychologist because she had this ability?

"I've been accepted at college," Mary Alice said in a rush.

Dr. Nyquist's expression did not change. "Oh?" she said. "At what college?"

"Bob Parker University," said Mary Alice. "It's in Tennessee."

The doctor nodded. "Yes, I know of it. Congratulations. It's an honor to be accepted by a college. But you don't seem happy about this news."

Mary Alice hesitated, then shook her head.

"Then you don't want to go there?"

Mary Alice thought about the letter, the feeling of dread she had had when her mother handed it to her. "I— guess not," she said.

"Can you tell me why you feel this way?"

Mary Alice's eyes went to the ceiling, finding again that aimless meandering crack in the plaster above her head. "It's far away," she said. "I've never been so far away. And it's—it's a religious school."

"Yes," said the doctor. "I believe it's affiliated with one of the evangelical churches. You don't want to go to a religious school then?"

Mary Alice shook her head.

"Perhaps you do not have to go there," Dr. Nyquist said matter-of-factly.

For a moment, with her eyes fixed on the ceiling, Mary Alice could almost accept the doctor's words. It sounded so simple.

Then she heard the doctor say, "But this is not easy for you, I'm afraid. Because of your parents?"

Mary Alice tried to imagine what it would be like telling her mother and father that she was not going to Bob Parker University after all. Her mother's unbelieving look. The hurt in her father's eyes. She could never do it.

"They're counting on it," she said. "They've been counting on it for three years."

"And you?"

"I—don't know," said Mary Alice.

She remembered the day when her father had first shown her the Bob Parker University catalog. It had come in the mail. He was always getting mail postmarked Knoxville, Tennessee, from Bob Parker the evangelist. He often watched Bob Parker's TV program early Sunday mornings too. Recently he had begun talking in his sermons about the things Bob Parker talked about: the Power of Prayer, the Healing of the Holy Spirit, the Miraculous Multiplication of Assets Invested in the Lord. Mary Alice didn't understand it. Her father seemed to be moving away from his preoccupation with sin and the impending Day of Judgment into a new kind of religion. Bob Parker's evangelism was more optimistic, but just as confusing to Mary

Alice, with its emphasis on slogans and mystical experiences. Bob Parker University, which had been Bob Parker's lifelong dream, had just opened. With the catalog came a color brochure showing Bob Parker himself standing between Billy Graham and the governor of Tennessee at the dedication ceremonies. The catalog was printed on shiny paper and on the cover it had a picture of the chapel, a gleaming white marble building that soared upward, seemingly straight to Heaven. The other buildings pictured inside were like that too—all massive and white with unlikely modern shapes and a lot of fountains and reflecting pools. They made Mary Alice feel uncomfortable. They were not quite real—they reminded her of Disneyland or perhaps the movie set for a film about the future. Whoever had designed them didn't seem to have had people in mind. Mary Alice could not imagine herself there, sitting on the perfectly trimmed grass next to one of the fountains or reading a book in the huge mushroom-shaped library.

Her father, though, thought it was beautiful. He talked about Bob Parker University with an animation he rarely displayed outside of the pulpit on Sunday mornings. "Have you ever seen such a campus, Mary Alice?" he exclaimed. "Just imagine going to school in such an inspiring setting. Be sure that you read the introduction, 'Why Bob Parker University?' It's a whole new idea in education, the education of the total Christian man or woman. This is the kind of college we need today, with the forces of sin so strong in the world. I feel sure that more and more schools are going to follow Bob Parker's lead."

He posted the Bob Parker University catalog on the church bulletin board, and at the next meeting of the Youth Fellowship he talked to the high school kids about being sure to consider Bob Parker University when they thought about colleges. The seniors in the group—there were only three—listened carefully and nodded their heads. Not many young people in West Greenville were thinking about colleges though. If they were, it was most likely the state agricultural and technical school or the state teachers' college in Munson.

Mary Alice had been glad that she was only a freshman and didn't have to think about colleges yet. Something about Bob Parker University made her uneasy. It wasn't just the overpowering look of the buildings. It was the thought of turning herself over like a lump of clay to be molded—body, mind, and spirit—into a total Christian woman. Was that what she wanted to be? She didn't know what she wanted to be. Would she know by the time she was a senior? Would she ever know? Mary Alice found herself hoping vaguely that something would have changed by the time she was a senior. Herself or her father or Bob Parker University. Maybe the new college would not be a success and she wouldn't have to think about going there.

But Bob Parker University had been a success. A lot of people seemed to agree with her father that this was the kind of college that was needed today, and each new catalog showed more buildings going up. The latest, a structure that looked exactly like a large white onion, was the

College of Business. And Bob Parker University even had a good football team. Her father, who had never been interested in sports, watched the whole game the Saturday that Bob Parker played Kentucky State on national television.

By that time someone from the church was attending Bob Parker University. Sherri Pinkerton, daughter of the building contractor who had gotten the shingles for the new church roof, had decided to go there as soon as she heard about the school. Sherri Pinkerton, tiny and blond and cute, the kind of girl who would be a cheerleader at whatever college she attended. Why had she chosen Bob Parker University? Mary Alice wondered. How could she know so positively what she wanted? But Mary Alice never asked her. She just listened while Sherri, home for Easter recess, told the Youth Fellowship all about the wonders of Bob Parker University—the beautiful dormitories, the fabulous teachers, the incredible commitment to Christ of everyone on campus.

By now Mary Alice was almost finished with her junior year, and it was time to be thinking about colleges. And she still didn't know what to do. She was going to college, of course. Everyone in her mother's and father's families had always gone to college. But where?

Her mother and father assumed that she was going to Bob Parker University. They had talked about the school so much in the last couple of years that gradually, without anyone ever actually saying so, it had become understood that she was going there. Mary Alice wasn't quite sure how it had happened. She knew she had never said she wanted to go, but she had never said she didn't want to either. She had never really said anything at all, just nodded and kept eating her dinner while her mother and father went on and on about the latest marvelous developments at Bob Parker University.

When Mary Alice thought about going there, something inside of her tightened up and she began to get the feeling of being closed in, of struggling to find air. But if she didn't go to Bob Parker University, where would she go? Only three other girls in her class were planning to go to college. Rosalie Hicks and Marlene Dwyer were both talking about living at home and going to Munson State, the teachers' college. Mary Alice didn't think she would want to live at home and go to college. Her friend Katie was going to Michigan State, where her father had gone and near to where a lot of her relatives lived. It would be nice to go to the same college as Katie, not to have to go all alone. But Michigan State was so big. She felt that she would be lost there if Katie left her for a minute to visit her relatives. And it was so far away that she probably wouldn't be able to come home for vacations.

There were other colleges, of course. There were hundreds of colleges all over the country. There was an all-girls school, she knew, in the same town as Peter's all-boys school. Only Peter wasn't sure whether he would still be there next year. He was hoping to go to MIT for graduate work. And anyway Mary Alice didn't think she wanted to go to an all-girls school. She felt sure somehow that if she did, there wouldn't be a chance of her ever having a date with a boy.

One day after school she went to the library and sat in a faraway corner where Mrs. Simmons, the librarian, wouldn't see what she was doing, and looked at college catalogs. The West Greenville library didn't have very many, and some of the ones they had were a few years old, but it was nice to look at all the pictures of ivy-covered bell towers and snow-covered statues and students reading under the shade of towering old trees. That was the kind of college she wanted to go to, she decided. One that was in the country and not too big and had a pretty campus. For some reason it seemed important that it have a pretty campus. It didn't matter so much what courses it offered, since she didn't know what she wanted to study anyway. As long as it had a school of liberal arts. She picked out three colleges that she liked the looks of: William and Mary in Virginia, which was kind of far away though not as far away as Michigan State but looked so beautiful with its old colonial buildings; Cornell, which was much closer and also had old-looking brick buildings with ivy growing all over everything; and St. Lawrence University, which wasn't quite as pretty but was smaller and looked quiet and friendly somehow from the pictures in the catalog. But then she decided against Cornell because it was too big.

She came home from the library, and before she had a chance to think about it and change her mind, she said to her mother, "I've been thinking that I'd like to apply to a couple of other colleges besides Bob Parker University."

Mary Alice's mother stopped in the middle of peeling a potato, a small frown appearing in the center of her forehead. "But I thought it was all settled that you are going to Bob Parker. I thought you wanted to. And your father is counting on it so much."

Mary Alice felt herself retreating, tempted to fold up altogether in the face of her mother's superior will. But she managed to say, her voice fading, losing its force, "Well, you are supposed to apply to at least three schools. In case you don't get into your first choice."

"I see," said your mother. "Yes, I'm sure that's a good idea in most cases." She turned back to the sink, her fingers flying over the potato once again. "But I don't think you need to worry about getting into Bob Parker University. Your grades are good. And I'm sure Sherri Pinkerton will write you a fine recommendation. And your father being a minister should be helpful too. I really don't think there's a thing to worry about. But you can talk to your father about it at dinner."

At dinner Mary Alice decided not to talk to her father about it after all. He was in one of his faraway moods, his jaw working absently on his pork chop and mashed potatoes while his mind worked on some other, far more important matter. His sermon for Sunday perhaps. It was Thursday night.

But her mother said, "Mary Alice has been wondering if she should apply to some other colleges besides Bob Parker University. Just in case she doesn't get in, you know. They advise them at school to have two or three other choices to fall back on."

Her father brought himself back with some effort from wherever he had been, looking at Mary Alice for a moment as if he had forgotten who she was.

"Well," he said, focusing on her finally, "I don't see why you need to do that. You will be accepted at Bob Parker University—I have faith that you will. And it costs money to apply to these colleges, money that isn't refunded if you decide not to go there. We really can't afford to be sending out money like that. Also, you know Bob Parker offers scholarship help for sons and daughters of ministers. What colleges were you thinking of applying to, anyway?"

Her father's eyes were fastened on hers now, and all at once the whole idea seemed ridiculous to her. She didn't know anything about those colleges, William and Mary and St. Lawrence University. You didn't choose a college— a place to spend four years of your life—by pretty pictures in a catalog. It was absurd. She wished she had never said anything about it at all.

But her father's eyes were still on hers, waiting for an answer. She looked down at her plate and said, her voice muffled as if her mouth were full of food, "I don't know. No college in particular."

So she didn't apply to any other colleges. She stopped thinking about it, in fact. For several months she didn't think about college at all. In the fall she sent in her application to Bob Parker University, filling in all the blank spaces on the application form very neatly and enclosing a five-page history of her life and spiritual development which her mother helped her outline on the back of a church bulletin. Her father took it to the post office on a Saturday morning. And by lunchtime she was in bed with the stomach flu.

She couldn't go to church the next morning. Her mother hovered over her, trying to decide whether it was more important to stay with Mary Alice in case she got worse or be in church so that she could lead the meeting of the Flower Committee after the service. Finally she decided that Mary Alice's condition was stable, and after surrounding her with pillows, magazines, and a glass of warm ginger ale to sip on, she hurried off to get Julia dressed for Sunday school.

A few minutes later the three of them left for church. Mary Alice lay in bed, not touching the ginger ale or the magazines or the algebra homework she had planned to do, just listening to how quiet the house was. She was aware of a feeling of relief—and immediately felt guilt at the relief—that she didn't have to go to church. She had always gone to church, just about every Sunday of her life as far back as she could remember. And next year at Bob Parker University she would go to church too. Everyone at Bob Parker University went to church at least once on Sunday and some of them went twice.

Mary Alice felt her teeth clench tightly together. She suddenly had a vision of herself at the dinner table that night months ago talking about colleges. Only she wasn't mumbling into her plate but speaking out clearly, not afraid that she wouldn't be able to put her thoughts into words or that she would hurt her father's feelings, because it was her life they were talking about, not his. "I'm sorry," she said calmly but firmly, "but I'm not going to Bob Parker University. It isn't what I want. I don't know yet what I do want, but I know Bob Parker is not the right college for me. I don't want to go to a religious school. I've been surrounded all my life by religion, and I don't really understand it or know what I believe in, or even if I believe in any of it at all. I need to get away from it now, to go to a school where I'll be left alone to figure things out for myself."

They would look at her in astonishment. Her father would look at her. There would be disappointment in those pale eyes and—yes—anger. He would not understand and he would be angry. But she would remain calm; she would be prepared, so that his anger could not reach her. They would say everything they could, and she would wait quietly until they were finished and then she would tell them what she was going to do.

She was going to apply to William and Mary in Virginia, she would tell them, and to St. Lawrence University. She would use the money in her savings account for the application fees, the money her grandmother had sent her on Christmas and birthdays ever since she was a baby "for your college education." She would ask her parents to drive her to see the schools, but if they wouldn't, maybe Peter would, or maybe she could go by herself. She would handle everything else herself—the applications, the interviews, the five-page essays about her life. The colleges would be impressed by her maturity.

But if her parents said No, they wouldn't or couldn't pay for her to go to college anywhere but at Bob Parker University, she still wouldn't go there. She would take the money from her savings account—they would have to let her have it, it was her money—and she would go to whatever town or city Peter was living in and get a job and work her way through college at night.

Mary Alice thought about how it would be, working in a five-and-ten in the daytime, or maybe a coffee shop, then climbing the stairs to her tiny room on the top floor of a rooming house, where she would heat up a can of soup on a hot plate before hurrying off to her evening class.

And then the vision faded. Mary Alice was in her own room in West Greenville, and her parents would be home from church soon, and she knew with a terrible certainty that none of this was going to happen. Because she lacked what it took to make it happen. She was weak, soft, spineless. When faced with her father's eyes, she could do nothing but mumble into her plate.

She was going to Bob Parker University.

Dr. Nyquist had not said anything for the longest time. Mary Alice had almost forgotten she was there; she had been speaking more to herself than to the doctor.

Now the doctor's crisp voice cut through the fog swirling inside Mary Alice's head. "When faced with difficult choices," she said, "the easiest way out often seems to be to do nothing, to make no choice. But to do nothing is in fact making a choice. You chose to accede to your parents' wishes because you were afraid of their response if you acted independently."

"I guess so," said Mary Alice, her voice dull.

"You don't think they will allow you to be a separate person," the doctor went on quietly. "Isn't that it?"

Mary Alice looked down at the bedspread, at her hands stretched out there, pale thin hands lacking the strength even to grasp each other. She nodded.

There was silence. Mary Alice waited for the doctor to say something more, but she didn't. Perhaps this was all the time there was for today. She waited for the doctor to say the words.

Dr. Nyquist stirred in her chair. "There is something I would like you to think about," she said. Mary Alice looked up and saw that the doctor was smiling again, though her eyes were serious. "Imagine that you were to say No to your father. Imagine that you were able to find the strength to do it. What would be the worst thing that could happen?"

"The very worst thing," repeated the doctor softly. She didn't wait for an answer. Rising to her feet, she said, "And now I'm afraid that's all the time we have for today."

15

Mary Alice knew she could never be as smart as Peter. Not if she studied every minute of every day. Peter just seemed to know things without studying. He was interested in so many different things; he seemed to absorb facts through his skin.

Even so, Mary Alice did well in school. She learned to read by herself, before they taught her in first grade. She liked reading; it seemed to her a wonderful thing to be able to go somewhere far away and do something she had never thought of doing just by reading a book. Spelling was easy for her, and so was arithmetic. She did her homework every night and could answer any question if the teacher called on her, though she didn't often raise her hand. She got all A's on her report cards all the way through eighth grade. She didn't think of herself as smart, though. It was just that the work wasn't that hard, and she studied. Peter was the smart one in the family.

When he was a senior in high school, he got the highest possible score on the math part of the college boards and received a full-tuition scholarship to his first-choice school. He knew what field he wanted to go into and was thinking already about graduate schools. Her mother and father seemed a little bewildered that their son wanted to be an astrophysicist—no one but Peter quite understood what it was—but still they were proud of him.

It didn't seem possible to Mary Alice that Peter was actually going away. And yet there was his room with only his model airplanes left on top of the bookcase—his charts of the stars had been taken off the wall and most of his books and his models of the moon and planets were packed in boxes ready to leave for college the next day. His suitcases were lined up in the hallway. And there was Peter, standing in the doorway of her room in old jeans and bare feet, holding a world globe in his hand.

"I thought maybe you'd like to have this," he said. "It comes in handy in high school history classes."

Mary Alice nodded. She didn't know what to say. The

idea of his leaving was beginning to fill her with an inexplicable feeling of panic. If she opened her mouth she was afraid she might blurt out, "Don't go," which was ridiculous. So she didn't say anything.

Peter seemed to sense what she was thinking. He reached out a finger and touched the globe so it spun slowly around. "One thing you have to remember when you live in this house, Mary Alice," he said. "It's a big world out there. And it won't be too long until you'll be taking this same trip out of here. So don't let them get you down. Do you know what I mean?"

Mary Alice nodded again. Somehow, without ever talking very much, she and Peter always understood each other.

"I don't know about this Bob Parker stuff that Dad's getting into now," Peter went on, frowning. "It sounds like a lot of hocus-pocus to me. Be careful not to let them shove it down your throat, okay? I mean, you've got to start doing your own thinking now that you're going into high school. Buck the tide. It's hard work—they've got a strong tide going—but it's got to be done."

He shifted from one foot to the other. "Well, I've got one more suitcase to pack. Guess I'd better get to it." He set the globe down on her desk, grinning. "Don't say I never gave you anything. It's not everyone who is given the world."

Peter turned to leave, then stopped in the doorway.

"Oh, one more thing," he said. "If they start to get you down, you can always write to me. Or call. I understand this fancy school has phones right in the room. Okay?"

Mary Alice tried to smile back at him. "Okay," she said.

"Don't forget," said Peter.

And then he was gone. In the weeks that followed, Mary Alice often thought about what he had said. She even started some letters to him, but she stopped as soon as she'd written the first few sentences. *Dear Peter: I am miserable. Without you here, I feel all alone in this family. . . . Dear Peter: I thought about what you said about bucking the tide. But I can't. I'm not like you. . . . Dear Peter: I hate this town. Why did we have to move here? I will never have a friend in this town. . . .* What good would it do to tell Peter all these things? What could he do about it? It was foolish to write to him.

But she felt so strange without him. He had always been there, positioned somehow between her and the outside world, kind of like a protective shield. When Peter was nearby, it didn't seem quite so hard to walk into a new school. Or to answer the questions of strangers after church. When Peter was there, she didn't get that sinking feeling in the pit of her stomach listening to her father rave on at the dinner table about receiving the joys of the Holy Spirit. "Mumbo-jumbo alakazam," he would whisper out of the side of his mouth, and she was able to smile and shrug. Peter kept her in balance. Without him she felt as if she were falling off the edge of something.

One night about a month after Peter had gone, Mary Alice was helping her mother do the dishes after supper.

They had just gotten a letter from Peter, saying that he needed more money for textbooks. "Those colleges," her mother sighed. "Seems like every time you turn around, it's more money for this or that. I tell you, if Peter hadn't gotten that scholarship, I don't know how we would have managed. The cost of college these days is out of sight. For a minister's family, it's almost prohibitive." She rinsed out the frying pan and handed it to Mary Alice to dry, her eyes lingering on her a moment before she picked up the next dish. "You know, Mary Alice," she said, starting to scrub again, "it's not too early for you to be thinking about college too. I know you've just started high school, but it's important to keep your grades up. You are smart. You may be able to qualify for a scholarship too."

Mary Alice was startled. It was the first time she could remember that either of her parents had ever commented on her intelligence, one way or another. All this time that she had been bringing home report cards with A's on them, they had looked and smiled and seemed vaguely pleased. But they had never really said anything. A's were what they were used to seeing on report cards. A's were what Peter always got.

That night when she was in bed, and at odd moments during the next day, her mother's words came back to her. "You are smart." The thought lit a tiny fire somewhere deep inside of her, warming her. But then she pushed it away. She was not smart. It was Peter who was smart. Her mother had just said that to make sure she studied now that she was beginning high school. Because she was worried about paying for college. Mary Alice could never win a full-tuition scholarship like Peter had done.

Yet the thought kept returning, creeping back stealthily after she had sent it away. Maybe it was true. Suppose it was. She didn't have to be as smart as Peter. She didn't need to score highest on a math test. She could be smart in different ways.

And it seemed to her suddenly that she was. The work that never seemed that hard for her was hard for other people in her class. Especially here in West Greenville. They were doing work in ninth grade that she had already done in eighth grade in Clinton. If she didn't study at all, she might not get A's, but she would still do well. The reason was that she was smart. Not brilliant like Peter. But smart.

Mary Alice came to believe it. She kept this new knowledge hidden away yet close by, taking it out late at night in the dark to examine it, savor it, nurture the small flame so that it burned brighter and stronger. There was something special about her after all. She who had never been called pretty, who lacked the ability to make people laugh or even take much notice of her, who had no special talents in art or music or anything else, who never got chosen for a sports team until next to last. She was smart.

She carried her secret—she thought it had to remain a secret, for who would she talk to about it?—with her as she walked to her classes through the wide unfamiliar halls of West Greenville High. It didn't seem to matter quite so much that she was alone, that she would never have any friends here because no one would ever see her in these loud, crowded halls filled with tall boys in football jackets. She would study and she would win a scholarship—maybe even a full-tuition scholarship—to a fine school and go on like Peter to some wonderful career.

She studied, coming home from school every day and sitting right down to do her homework. And she continued to get all A's. Her mother was pleased; even her father seemed to be paying attention when he looked at her first report card. "Very nice work, Mary Alice," he said, and he looked straight at her, not somewhere over her shoulder as he did when he was thinking of something else. And for an instant, so fleeting that she wasn't sure she had seen it, he smiled. At school she was starting to feel not quite so much a stranger. Her teachers called on her often, confident that she would know the answers when no one else did. And the other kids knew her name now, sometimes stopping her in the hall to ask about the homework assignment. And, miraculously, she had a friend.

Mary Alice had always disliked gym. It was the one class where no matter how hard she worked, she never did well. Sports didn't come naturally to her. The parts of her body didn't seem to know how to work together properly. She had never failed gym; no one failed if they appeared to be trying. But she had never gotten more than an "Average" on her report card. She didn't mind gym class so much on days when they did things like high jumping or tumbling on mats on the gym floor. She would never do it quite right, but at least it was over quickly, and then it was someone else's turn, and she could stand in line and watch. The thing about gym that she really disliked was when they chose teams. It seemed like they were always having to choose teams for soccer or volleyball or basketball or softball. Mary Alice would hear the teacher say it, and her mouth would feel dry. Her stomach would begin to shrink inside her, and then it would seem as if her whole body were growing smaller. She would look away, down at the floor, not looking up again until it was all over. Maureen Daly would always be chosen first (in Clinton it had been Josie Pagano), and next would be Michele Bennett, who was very tall, and then would come the rest of the class, the in-between ones, and finally there would be just three or four of them left sitting on the hard shiny gym floor. Mary Alice's stomach would have contracted into a hard knot by the time there were only two of them left, she and Katie Atkinson. Katie Atkinson, not exactly fat but round-looking—a small round person. Even her glasses were round and too big for her face, giving her an owlish appearance. She had a way of moving lethargically, as if her batteries had worn down. Then someone would say, without enthusiasm, "I'll take Mary Alice." And the other team would be left with Katie. Only sometimes it was the other way, and Mary Alice was the last one chosen.

She found that she couldn't look at Katie Atkinson.

She avoided sitting near her in gym class, and afterward, when they were getting dressed in the locker room, she avoided dressing near her. It was as if there was some strange contest between them, one that neither of them wanted but that they could not control. Even when she passed Katie Atkinson in the hall, Mary Alice felt uncomfortable. She always looked the other way so she wouldn't have to say hello.

But then one day, sitting on the floor with only the two of them left again, feeling the cold draft making goose bumps on her bare legs while she waited, she heard a muffled choking sound. She looked over, and at first she thought Katie Atkinson was getting sick. But then she saw that she was smiling, trying to stifle a giggle. Without thinking about it, Mary Alice smiled back. And suddenly they were friends.

After gym, standing next to Katie at the mirror combing her hair, Mary Alice asked, "What were you laughing about in gym?" And Katie answered, "I don't know. It just seemed silly all of a sudden, to care if you're picked last for a volleyball game. Like I was planning to go on and play in the Olympics or something."

Mary Alice laughed then, a strange high-pitched laugh that didn't sound like her at all and seemed to go on too long, almost out of control. She felt giddy with relief and excitement. She had a friend in West Greenville.

They walked home together that afternoon, and every day after that. They studied together, sometimes at Mary Alice's house and sometimes at Katie's house. Mary Alice liked to go to Katie's house, it was so different from her own. It was a big white house, very pretty on the outside—Katie's father was vice president of the First National Bank, the red brick bank on Main Street—but inside it was messy and noisy. Katie's younger sister and brother and their friends and a big black dog named Grover were always running in and out, shouting and dropping books and clothes and roller skates. Katie's mother didn't seem to care. She sat in the middle of the confusion reading magazines and drinking coffee, and once a week a cleaning lady came in to straighten up the house. Katie's mother was always home. That was because she didn't belong to any organizations. "She says she doesn't like ladies in groups," Katie explained. It wasn't clear to Mary Alice what Katie's mother did with all the time she didn't spend cleaning or going to meetings. She seemed to read a lot. And when she was in the mood, she cooked up big batches of cookies or brownies or even homemade bread. And she talked. She talked to the mailman and the cleaning lady and all the children who kept running in and out. Once Mary Alice even saw her on the floor with Katie's nine-year-old brother, Michael, and his friend Teddy trying to figure out how to make a kite. It was strange, but nice.

"What church do they belong to?" Mary Alice's mother asked after Katie had visited Mary Alice's house for the first time. "Methodist," said Mary Alice. "But they don't go to church very often. Katie's mother doesn't like to get up early on weekends." Mary Alice's mother frowned at this, and Mary Alice decided not to tell her what Katie had said about her mother not liking ladies in groups. Always after that it seemed as if there was a faint hint of disapproval in Mary Alice's mother's voice when she spoke about Katie's mother. But she seemed to like Katie.

Katie had already decided what she was going to do after she graduated from high school. She was going to Michigan State like her father and then to medical school to become a doctor. She loved science. She reminded Mary Alice of Peter, she was so sure of where she was going.

It seemed to Mary Alice that it was time she figured out what her career was going to be too. She thought about it a lot during the summer after her freshman year. She could see now that it wasn't going to be in science or math. Those were the subjects she found the hardest, the ones she had to struggle with in order to get A's. English was probably her best subject, but she also liked history, especially when it wasn't about wars or debates in Congress but about how people lived a long time ago. And she liked art too, even though she wasn't particularly good at it. She thought vaguely of being a teacher of something, art or English or American history. Or maybe a kindergarten teacher. She liked the idea of teaching very little kids, before they got to knowing too much and talking back.

Then she started school again and got Mrs. Davidson for sophomore English. Everyone said Mrs. Davidson was a good teacher, but Mary Alice wasn't prepared for the effect she would have on her. Mrs. Davidson was a small, very thin lady with steel-gray hair piled in a ball on top of her head. She spoke in a quiet, rather hesitant voice so that it was easy not to listen to her, to think instead about the test coming up in geometry next period or what you were going to do after school. But if you listened you couldn't help being aware that Mrs. Davidson loved American literature. She would read aloud from Robert Frost or Edgar Allan Poe or F. Scott Fitzgerald and her voice would gradually gain force and on her face would be an expression of pure happiness. It was contagious. Before Mary Alice realized it, she found herself straining to hear every word, and hearing words in an entirely new way. The way some words had a sharp sting to them while others soothed, the way just three or four words could create an image more vivid than a painting, the way words could be put together in various rhythms that ebbed and flowed like music. Her father used words like this in his sermons, she realized. In some odd way her father had a connection to these writers of American literature.

After several weeks in Mrs. Davidson's class Mary Alice found herself longing one night to write something herself. Perhaps this was the way to capture the inexpressible thoughts that seemed often to float just out of reach somewhere inside her head. She got a pencil and paper and she sat cross-legged on her bed and tried to write a poem. She soon found it too difficult—half-remembered rules about rhyme and meter kept intruding—so instead she just wrote down combinations of words, fragments that she might use some day in a poem or story. "Quiet quivering dawn." "The moon meandering." (She had always liked using words together that started with the same sound: alliteration, it was called according to Mrs. Davidson.) "Wind weaving and dancing through dry leaves." "A smiling face empty inside." "An old man made out of paper and bone."

She didn't know where these bits and pieces came from or what she might do with them. They just seemed to pop into her consciousness at odd moments, mostly late at night, and she would write them down in her notebook. She had bought a notebook at the five-and-ten, the kind with a green marble-looking cover. She kept it hidden under her sweaters in her bottom drawer, and she didn't tell anyone about it, not even Katie. She felt that she was storing up the contents of the notebook for something, that someday she would know what it was for. The fragments grew longer; two or three seemed on their way to becoming poems, and one was the beginning of a story about a girl and her dog, a big black dog named Grover.

In January Mrs. Davidson assigned a book report. It could be on any book by any of the writers they had talked about in class. Mary Alice went to the library and took out *For Whom the Bell Tolls* by Ernest Hemingway. Hemingway was her favorite of all the authors whose stories Mrs. Davidson had read aloud. She was fascinated by the way he could say so much in so few—and such ordinary—words, and she liked the lean, hard sound of his writing, which matched the subjects he wrote about. It seemed to create a poetry of its own, though it wasn't poetry. When she started reading *For Whom the Bell Tolls,* Mary Alice found herself being drawn into—and soon totally immersed in—a different world, the world of Robert Jordan and the Spanish Civil War, a war she hadn't even heard of so far in history class. She couldn't stop reading the book. For the three days it took to finish it she walked around in a daze, seeing everything around her as shadowy and unreal, her real life taking place high in the sunny mountains of Spain with Robert Jordan.

She finished the book and for a day afterward could do nothing. The book reverberated in her head; she still saw the colors and heard the sounds, even smelled the fragrant pine needles under her feet. She sat down to write her book report and thought that she couldn't do it. The book was too much a part of her; she couldn't get far enough away from it to write a book report. But then she started, and amazingly it came. She wrote the whole report without stopping, feeling it flow effortlessly like she sometimes felt words flowing into her green notebook late at night, as if they had just been waiting somewhere for her to write them down. When she was finished, she read it over and hardly recognized it as her own writing. It was good, she thought, very good. She was a writer. It struck her, with a rush of excitement, that that was what she was going to be.

As soon as she had handed in the paper to Mrs. Davidson, though, she began to have doubts. It was so different from other people's book reports, from other book reports she had written. What if it wasn't really any good? What if she had just been carried away by the book and had written a lot of foolish nonsense? She was embarrassed now, afraid to look at Mrs. Davidson and find out what she thought of the book report.

But when she got the paper back, three interminable days later, there was an *A* in the upper right-hand corner in Mrs. Davidson's neat red pencil. And underneath she had written: "An excellent report. Some very fine writing here. And you show a good understanding of the structure and theme of the book. Please see me after class."

Mary Alice felt her face grow warm. It had been good writing, "very fine writing," in fact. She was embarrassed again to look at Mrs. Davidson; she felt her pleasure showing like nakedness. She looked down at the paper and read again the teacher's comments. Why, she wondered, did Mrs. Davidson want to see her after class? Maybe to tell her again what a fine book report it was, to ask if she could read it aloud to the class, maybe even to encourage Mary Alice to show her more of her writing, to tell her she had talent.

She went up to Mrs. Davidson's desk when class was over and stood, looking down at her books, while Mrs. Davidson spoke to a couple of other students about reading assignments. When the room was finally empty, Mrs. Davidson said, "Sit down, Mary Alice."

Mary Alice sat down, and Mrs. Davidson cleared her throat. She seemed uncomfortable, as if she hadn't quite made up her mind what she was going to say. Her face, which was usually as pale as the dull gray and brown suits that she wore, now was tinged with pink. Mary Alice knew suddenly that Mrs. Davidson wasn't going to tell her what a fine book report it was.

"I wanted to talk to you about your book report," Mrs. Davidson began in her usual quiet voice, looking down at the papers on her desk instead of at Mary Alice. "As I wrote on the paper, it was a fine report. Unusually fine."

She looked up at Mary Alice and smiled, a forced smile, it seemed to Mary Alice.

Confused, Mary Alice nodded. "Thank you," she mumbled.

Mrs. Davidson looked down at her desk again. "The writing was quite remarkable for a high school sophomore. And quite different from your other reports. I wondered where you got your inspiration for it."

Mary Alice tried to think what Mrs. Davidson could mean. Was she referring to the way she had felt while she was reading *For Whom the Bell Tolls*? She didn't want to talk to Mrs. Davidson about that. It seemed too personal somehow. Finally she said, "It was the book that gave me the inspiration. I—I really liked the book."

Mrs. Davidson nodded. "Yes, I could tell that. Discovering Hemingway for the first time is an exciting experience. A real revelation. After you finished the book, did you read more about it? In some of the books of literary criticism in the library perhaps?"

All at once it came to Mary Alice what Mrs. Davidson

was getting at. Why she had wanted to see her after class. Mrs. Davidson didn't believe that she had written the book report herself. She thought she had plagiarized it, copied it from somewhere else.

Mary Alice felt a coldness grip her, an iciness deep in the pit of her stomach. "No," she said, almost in a whisper. "I didn't read anything else."

Mrs. Davidson was looking at her now, and her eyes were hard. She didn't look like the same Mrs. Davidson whose whole face lit up with joy every time she read aloud from Robert Frost.

Mary Alice looked back at her, struggling not to look away, not to give in to the urge to get up and run from the room. Then Mrs. Davidson would be sure of her guilt.

"I think—" began Mrs. Davidson and then stopped, evidently changing her mind. She abruptly began arranging the papers on her desk, putting them into piles as if she were getting ready to leave for the day. "That's all I wanted to tell you, Mary Alice," she said, and her voice seemed to have softened, though her eyes remained focused on her papers. "Just that it was an exceptional book report."

Mary Alice felt herself released suddenly. Relief flooded through her, and she stood up to go, then hesitated, thinking that she should say something. "Good night," she managed finally. "Thank you."

As she reached the door she heard Mrs. Davidson say, "Good night, Mary Alice. Have a good weekend."

Had there been something different in her voice? Mary

Alice wondered as she walked down the nearly empty hall. An edge that wasn't usually there? A hint of sarcasm? Mary Alice could not be sure. Had Mrs. Davidson believed her or hadn't she? When she got to her locker, she noticed that her hands were shaking so that she could hardly open it. She was glad to find that Katie had not waited for her. She didn't feel capable of talking to anyone now.

When she got home, she went right up to her room. Dropping her books, she lay down on her bed. She closed her eyes, shutting everything out, pulling down a curtain all around her. She lay very still, thinking of nothing. Little by little her mind seemed to drift away, out of her body, out of the room, to somewhere far away. Somewhere where everything was blue sky and sunshine and the sweet sharp smell of pine needles. And calm. So very calm.

After awhile she opened her eyes and she still felt calm. She sat up and reached for the notebook with the book report inside. Her hand wasn't shaking at all now.

Mary Alice started reading the book report. It didn't seem at all familiar to her; she felt she had never seen it before. As she read she began to understand what Mrs. Davidson had meant. The words didn't sound like hers. And yet she was sure they hadn't come from anywhere else. Then she realized where they had come from. They had come from Hemingway. She had been so absorbed by his book that, without knowing it, she had written her report in his style.

A feeling of shame swept over her. Mrs. Davidson had been right. Though it hadn't happened quite as she imagined, Mary Alice had plagiarized. Or was it plagiarizing? She hadn't meant to copy. She hadn't copied at all really. It was more as if by some strange process she had become, for a little while, the writer she admired. Why hadn't Mrs. Davidson seen that? And was it so bad? If the writing was good, couldn't she do something like it again, only in her own voice rather than Hemingway's?

She would ask Mrs. Davidson. She would explain to her exactly what had happened. Surely she would understand.

Mary Alice looked down again at the paper in her hand. It still looked unfamiliar; she couldn't even remember having written it. It had been a fluke. What would be the point of talking to Mrs. Davidson about it? She could never do it again. And she had no voice of her own.

Very carefully she folded the book report in half. She reached into her bottom drawer, under her sweaters, and found the green notebook. Stuffing the book report inside it, she closed the drawer and went downstairs.

She didn't look at the book report or the green notebook again for the rest of the year. Two other book reports were assigned and she wrote them, taking care that they sounded like everyone else's book reports, that nothing crept in that Mrs. Davidson might suspect came from somewhere else. Mrs. Davidson gave her a B+ on both papers and handed them back without comment. Neither she nor Mary Alice mentioned the Hemingway book report again. Sometimes Mary Alice thought she saw Mrs. Davidson looking at her in an odd way, and once or twice she was sure the teacher was going to say something to her, but she didn't. Mary Alice was glad. She didn't care anymore about the Hemingway book report. She couldn't seem to care anymore about English. All spring she sat in class while Mrs. Davidson read aloud from Willa Cather and Sherwood Anderson, and her mind kept wandering. Whatever it had been that had captured her attention, excited her, was gone.

At the end of the term she got a B+ in English, the first B ever on her report card. Mary Alice wondered what her parents would say when they saw it. But it turned out that her father hardly looked at her report card; he was caught up in a crisis about whether or not the church organist was going to leave for another church. And her mother only said, "A nice report card, dear. But you better work a little harder in English next time."

After that first B there were other B's. Math kept getting harder, and her physics teacher didn't bother explaining things to students who didn't understand right away. It was no longer clear to Mary Alice what the point was of working so hard just to see the letter *A* printed on a piece of paper. Where were these A's going to take her? She didn't even know where she wanted to go.

Also, in her junior year it became evident that boys didn't like girls who were too smart. Mary Alice didn't figure this out for herself; Katie told her. Somehow over the summer, when Mary Alice hadn't been looking, Katie had changed. She was still Mary Alice's friend and she was still going to be a doctor, but suddenly she was interested in boys. It was all she talked about almost, especially a boy named Carl Schumacher who played on the soccer team. Katie even looked different. Not her figure, which was still quite round, but her face. She had gotten new glasses over the summer which suited the shape of her face. And then her mother had taken her to Munson to have her hair cut. And all at once Katie looked pretty.

She started acting different too. In algebra class she didn't raise her hand anymore, even though Mary Alice knew that she still knew all the answers. And when there were boys around to hear, it seemed as if she was always making fun of herself, saying, "Now how does Miss Page think I can translate eight pages of French?" or "I just know I'm going to fail that history test," laughing, shaking her head, acting as if she had no brains whatsoever.

Mary Alice thought her behavior was very strange. Finally one day, waiting in the hall to go in to history class, she couldn't stand it anymore, and she said, "Don't be silly, Katie. You've never flunked a history test. We studied all those dates last night, remember?"

Katie gave her the worst look and didn't say another word. But later that afternoon, when they were doing their homework up in Mary Alice's room, Katie stopped in the middle of an algebra problem. Lying back with her arms under her head, she said, "Do you know what I figured out about boys, Mary Alice?"

"What?" said Mary Alice, not looking up from her book. Katie was always figuring out something new about boys.

"They don't like it when a girl can do anything better than they can. It really bothers them. Like sports, for example. It seems like they resent it when a girl is good at sports. They need to feel bigger and stronger than a girl in order to be comfortable with her."

"Mmm," said Mary Alice. It was true that boys didn't take out girls who were taller than they were or who could beat them at baseball like Maureen Daly.

"And smarter too," said Katie. "If they think you are too smart it makes them feel dumb. You can't let them think you are a brain or you'll never have any dates."

Mary Alice didn't think she would ever have any dates anyway. But she could see what Katie meant. There was a girl named Donna Sue Parks in the senior class, the daughter of the school principal. Everyone knew she was the smartest girl in the school—she had won all kinds of prizes and was a member of the National Honor Society and would probably win several full-tuition scholarships to college. But no one ever took her out on a date.

Katie sighed. "The worst thing is to be good in math. You know boys are supposed to be better than girls in math and science. It drives them crazy if you get better grades than they do."

Mary Alice looked over at Katie. She had never thought of that before. "But you have to do well in math and science if you're going to be a doctor."

"Exactly," said Katie. She took off her glasses, breathed on them, then polished them on Mary Alice's bedspread. "So what is a person to do?"

There didn't seem to be any answer to that question. "I don't know," Mary Alice said finally.

"Me either," said Katie with a shrug. After a minute she sat up and opened her algebra book again.

What Katie did was to keep on getting good grades in math and science at the same time she kept talking about how terribly she was doing. It seemed to work very well. None of the boys thought she was a brain. In fact a boy named Kenny Griffin who sat next to her in algebra even offered to help her with some of the problems she didn't understand. Katie said okay, since even though Kenny was nowhere near as good-looking as Carl Schumacher, he was still a boy.

Mary Alice couldn't pretend like Katie did. She didn't know how, for one thing, and she would have felt guilty saying things that weren't true. But she didn't want to be like Donna Sue Parks either. So she just stopped studying so hard. She convinced her mother that she should get a job after school working at the five-and-ten to earn money for clothes. And instead of all A's on her report card, she got a few A's and a few B's and even a C in physics. Her father frowned when he saw that, and her mother made a big fuss about maybe Mary Alice should get some tutoring and maybe she shouldn't have gotten an after-school job since it was interfering with her school work. So the last term she studied hard and got a B in physics.

Smart, but not too smart—that was how she thought of herself. She would never win a full-tuition scholarship like Peter. She felt a little regretful about that, and a little bit guilty that her parents would have to pay for college. But then, she wasn't going to the college of her choice like Peter was. She was going to Bob Parker University.

16

She was driving down a country road on her way to college. She was alone. Her father and mother were letting her drive to school by herself. There wasn't room for anyone else in the car anyway. It was piled high with the things she was taking with her: suitcases and clothes bags and boxes of books and curtains and a typewriter and a lamp and her ice skates. On top of everything in the back seat was her old faded Raggedy Ann doll. She wasn't quite sure why she was taking her Raggedy Ann doll to college. It seemed like a mistake.

She was driving by herself, but she knew the way. It was a road she'd been on many times before—the road to Peter's school. Peter's school had accepted her even though she was a girl. She was so happy to be going there and not to Bob Parker University that she kept smiling to herself as she drove down the road.

She thought that she ought to drive a little faster. The sun was going down, she noticed, and it was starting to get dark. Peter would be waiting for her. And she had never driven by herself after dark.

The trees seemed to fly by on either side as she went faster. She could hardly make them out; they were just blurred black shapes rushing past in the gray dusk. There didn't seem to be any houses along the road, or other cars. She was all alone. It occurred to her that maybe she had taken a wrong turn. Maybe she wasn't still on the road to Peter's school. But she couldn't go back. She had to keep on driving down that road.

Now the night was so dark that she couldn't see anything. A fine mist seemed to hang over the road ahead, like a wisp of cloud that had fallen from the sky. And then all at once she was inside of the cloud. It surrounded the car, wrapped it in a swirling curtain of fog. She felt as if she ought to be able to reach out and push back the curtain with her hands, but she couldn't. She was inside and she couldn't get out. She had to get out. She had to go fast and leave it behind.

She saw the road ahead curve to the left, and then there was no more road. It was swallowed up by fog. She tried to turn, but she was going too fast. She felt the car leaving the road, skidding, out of her control.

"No, no!" she cried out.

She heard herself crying. Wake up. She had to wake up. It was a dream. She could get away from it.

With an immense effort Mary Alice pulled herself away, forced her eyes open. Her heart was pounding; her skin was drenched in perspiration.

There was a yellow light somewhere in the darkness. She blinked at it.

It was the night light in the corridor. She was in bed, in the hospital. It had been a dream.

17

"Have you had any dreams?" the doctor asked.

Of course she knew.

"Yes," said Mary Alice.

"Can you tell me about it?"

She couldn't. It was too close. Already she felt the darkness and the terror creeping back. She couldn't let it. Not yet.

She shook her head.

"A bad dream. Do you have them often?"

Mary Alice nodded. "They are always different. But the same. About the—accident."

"Yes." The doctor's voice was soft, soothing. "Perhaps later you may want to talk about it."

Later. When she was ready.

In the meantime they talked about driving.

"I didn't know what it was going to be like, driving a car," said Mary Alice.

"What do you mean?" asked the doctor.

Driving a car gave her a feeling she had never had before. She was going somewhere. She, Mary Alice, going where she wanted to go, directing the huge powerful machine beneath her. She could stop anytime or turn left or right or keep pressing down on the accelerator until she was hurtling through space, a speeding object. She could even keep on going, out of town, out of her life to a new one somewhere. For the first time, she had the feeling of endless possibilities.

Of course, she mostly just drove in town, shopping or to Katie's house or to pick up Julia after her piano lesson. She couldn't waste gas. Her father always looked at the gas gauge when she brought the car back. But once in a while she would fill up the tank with the money she'd earned at her job at the five-and-ten, and then she and Katie would go for a ride.

They would drive around anywhere they felt like going. Katie liked to go to one of the nearby towns and look at houses. It was a favorite game of hers. She would look at all the houses and then choose the one she would live in when she was married and a doctor and had a lot of money. Mary Alice would play the game with her, but she didn't really like it. The big houses that Katie liked seemed overwhelming to her. Having so much space would make her feel small, alone. What did people do all day locked behind their wrought-iron gates and paneled doors? But then the small houses they passed, each one just like the ones on either side of it, depressed her too. How did people know who they were when their neighbor's house was exactly like theirs? And worst of all were the houses that sat right alongside the railroad tracks or next to a gas station surrounded by concrete, or the apartments over stores in the middle of downtown. She couldn't live in a place like that. She knew she couldn't. The noise, the hemmed-in feeling, the ugliness of it would press down on her until finally it would crush her.

She didn't know why it mattered so much. People lived in all kinds of places, much worse than any she had seen, and they survived, even seemed happy. Why couldn't she? Why was she so fragile that she could only live in a certain kind of house? She had the feeling that her life was precariously balanced. A wrong move, a wrong choice, and it would all topple over.

But then somehow it was different when she was driving. Out of town, driving fast down an unknown country road, going nowhere in particular. That was what she liked. She would feel a surge of hope. Everything was stretched out in front of her—fields and flowers, rolling green valleys, distant hills, all bright with sunshine. She could go anywhere. Surely she would find the right place. It was there, somewhere out in front of her. It had to be.

Sometimes unexpectedly she had the urge just to keep on driving. Not to turn back on the road to West Greenville, but to take whatever road she was on and keep going until it ended and then take some other road she had never seen before and keep going until—what? She didn't know. But the urge was so strong that she almost could not resist it. She had to clench her teeth together and tell herself to slow down, lift her foot from the accelerator to the brake, get ready to turn right, come on now, do it, before Katie started asking what was wrong with her.

"I guess what it was about driving," said Mary Alice slowly, "was that it made me feel free. As if I could go wherever I wanted."

"As if you, rather than your parents, were in control of your life?"

"Yes," said Mary Alice.

The doctor smiled.

18

Her job at the five-and-ten gave her kind of the same feeling. She was doing something on her own. At the end of the week she got a little envelope with money in it. It wasn't much money—she was only working Saturday mornings and two afternoons a week after school—but it was hers to spend any way she wanted.

Mostly she spent it on clothes. That was why she had gotten the job, so she could buy her own clothes.

For a long time Mary Alice hadn't cared about clothes. She had gotten used to wearing whatever her mother brought home from all the rummage sales and school sales and tag sales she went to. And the things her mother sewed for her herself. Her mother would come home with a pattern and some material she had found on sale and ask Mary Alice how she liked it. "Fine," Mary Alice would always say, whether she liked it or not. If her mother was going to go to the trouble of sewing something for her, it didn't seem right to complain. And anyway, it didn't really matter. What difference did it make what she wore?

But then, in the second half of her junior year, suddenly it did make a difference. Shortly after Katie had discovered boys, Katie discovered clothes. She spent hours looking through fashion magazines, deciding what styles would do the most for her figure. And she was always wanting to stop in at Pearl's Department Store after school just to see if they had gotten in anything new. Mary Alice thought Katie was really getting carried away. And yet after awhile she couldn't help looking at her own clothes in a different way. It struck her all at once that they were awful.

The clothes that her mother got at rummage sales were always a couple of years out of style. When the other girls at school were wearing layers, Mary Alice was wearing ruffles. After they switched to ruffles, she was wearing layers. And the skirts were never the right length. Even the clothes that her mother made never seemed to fit quite right. They would be too loose here or too tight there, or they hung funny. And her mother always chose material that was dark, somber-looking. Her favorite color was dark green. Mary Alice seemed to have a closet full of dark green clothes.

When Mary Alice realized what she had been wearing all this time, she was horrified. No wonder boys didn't talk to her or even seem to know she existed. If they ever thought of her at all, it was probably as that girl with the funny clothes. And the girls too. They probably laughed about it when she wasn't around. Imagine coming to school dressed like that. What could she have been thinking of?

The day she got her first pay envelope, she went across the street to Pearl's with Katie and bought a new skirt, a blue plaid. The next week she bought a blouse to go with it. And that was all she wore after that, the same skirt and blouse every day until she had saved enough money to buy a sweater. The rest of her clothes hung in her closet untouched, limp reminders of the person she used to be. Little by little she pushed them to the back so she wouldn't have to look at them. She didn't feel able to tell her mother, but she knew she would never wear any of them again.

At first she worried about how her parents would react to her new clothes. But they hardly seemed to notice, they were both so busy with her father's new Lenten Bible study course and preparations for the Spring Fair. Only once, when she wore her new red sweater for the first time, did she feel her father's eyes on her at the break-fast table. "Let the women adorn themselves not with braided hair or gold or pearls or costly array, but with good works," he said, a frown creasing his forehead. Mary Alice decided not to buy anything else that was red.

If it hadn't been for needing the clothes, she probably wouldn't have applied for the job at the five-and-ten. The whole thing was too scary. The idea of waiting on people she didn't know, finding out what they wanted, figuring out the sales tax, giving back the right change was scary. Even talking to Mr. Fishman, the manager of the store, was scary. Mary Alice sat across the desk from him in his tiny office on a balcony at the back of the store while he looked over her application. He was a small, sour-looking man with very white skin and very black hair. He reminded Mary Alice of a fish, a fish trapped in a bowl. He looked as if he had lived all his life in the five-and-ten. Mr. Fishman didn't say a word while he read the application, but finally he put it down and stared at Mary Alice.

I'm not qualified, thought Mary Alice. I should never have applied for the job.

"Can you work nights before Christmas?" asked Mr. Fishman abruptly.

"I—I guess so," stammered Mary Alice.

"All right. You start next week. Be on time, no fooling around."

That was it. It was the longest conversation Mary Alice ever had with Mr. Fishman. He ran the five-and-ten as if it were some fancy department store, darting around checking display windows, rearranging counters, yelling at the stock boy to get that merchandise upstairs right away, frowning at the salesclerks if they talked to each other or came in a minute late. He never smiled and he never said good night.

But despite Mr. Fishman and despite her own doubts Mary Alice found that she liked the job. Once she got the hang of operating the cash register, ringing up sales and making change was fun. She even liked choosing the right size bag, dropping in the merchandise, and carefully stapling it closed. But the most surprising thing was the way she felt standing behind the counter talking to customers. She actually enjoyed it. Something about being on the inside looking out, being not Mary Alice Fletcher but the salesclerk on the stationery counter, gave her courage. She found herself talking to everyone, answering questions, making suggestions. "May I help you?" she would ask. "Yes, we do have embroidery thread. It's on counter seven right over there, next to the knitting wool. And garden supplies are on counter ten next to the wall. There's a spring special on gardening gloves this week." Mature, capable, smiling, friendly, she seemed to be a different person.

After the first few weeks Mr. Fishman put her on the toy counter, and that was the best place to work of all. Some of her customers were aunts or grandmothers, and Mary Alice would ask how old the child was and suggest a gift that she or he might like. But mostly they were children. A boy would come in clutching a handful of coins in a dirty fist, and she would watch while he circled the counter, picking up toys and putting them down, unable to make up his mind. After a few minutes she would ask, "How much money do you have to spend?" and the child would drop the sticky collection of coins in her hand. "Eighty-seven cents," she would say. "Did you see the racing cars over here for fifty-nine cents? If you got one of those, you would have a little bit left over for some gum or something." Sometimes it took a long time, but eventually the child would run off happily, waving his package in his hand, to show his mother what he had bought. Mary Alice felt pleased with herself, as if she personally were responsible for his happiness. She came to have a proprietary feeling about the toy counter. It was hers. She took pride in straightening out the merchandise, dusting off the boxes that had been there a while, putting out a new display, arranging it so that the toys the little kids liked best were where they could reach them.

She could see now how Mr. Fishman could take the store so seriously. Maybe she would have a store someday. She didn't know which part of the job she liked more—tending to the merchandise or talking to the children.

But then why was it that it was at her job that things first began to go wrong?

It started with a bottle of perfume. Mary Alice had never had any perfume—it was one of those things that her father and mother didn't really approve of—but for weeks Katie had been talking about this kind advertised on TV that smelled different on everyone who wore it and

was absolutely certain to make boys froth at the mouth
when they smelled it. Mary Alice had decided to buy
some when she got her pay envelope on Friday. She had
the money in her purse and had just walked over to the
cosmetics counter when Marge, the clerk, said to her,
"Mind the store for me a minute, will you, honey? I've
got to get my cashbox from the office."

Mary Alice stood there looking down at the perfume
display. Hardly any customers were left in the store. It
was closing time. She picked up the small-sized bottle of
perfume, then looked at the middle-sized one made of
blue glass shaped like a flower. She couldn't decide which
to buy. And then, without having the slightest idea that
she was going to do it, she dropped the small bottle into
her purse.

She stood absolutely still, paralyzed by what she had
done. Why had she done it? She had the money right
there to pay for the perfume. She had been planning to
buy it. And then she was aware of someone walking very
quietly up behind her. Mr. Fishman. Oh, please, God,
don't let it be Mr. Fishman. But it was only Marge,
shuffling back in the bedroom slippers she always wore at
work.

"Thanks, honey," she said cheerfully. "Why don't you
scoot on home now? And have a nice weekend."

Mary Alice couldn't answer. She raised her hand in a
feeble wave and walked toward the door.

By the time she got home, she was convinced that she
had just imagined taking the perfume. It wouldn't be in

her purse. It couldn't be. But when she looked through her purse, way in the bottom, she found it, a slim vial of sickly-looking pale yellow liquid.

She didn't even open it to see how it smelled. She just shoved it into her top drawer, way at the back where her mother might not notice it. If she did, Mary Alice would tell her Katie had given it to her. She knew she could never wear it. It had been a mistake, a terrible mistake. But she had been lucky no one had seen her. And it would never happen again.

Only it did happen again. About two weeks later. It was a scarf this time, a pink flowered scarf. And a few days after that, a bracelet.

It was like a disease. Mary Alice would be looking down at something on the counter and she would feel it coming on, like an attack of some kind of fever. She would begin to feel hot and her skin would crawl, as if she were about to break out in a rash. And then something would compel her, her heart pounding and her knees shaking, to reach down and close her hand around whatever it was. Within seconds it would be in her pocket or her purse. She didn't know where she got the cunning to do it so easily: the sidelong glance to see that the clerk was busy elsewhere, the quick sure movements of her hands. She, a minister's daughter, a person who had never been quick at anything else, seemed to have been born with the ability to steal.

She felt awful all the time she was doing it, and she

felt awful afterward. She didn't want the things after she had taken them. She didn't even want to look at them. She couldn't bear to wear them, and she couldn't think of how to get rid of them. So she stuffed them in her closet and her bureau drawers, waiting for the day when her mother would find them and ask, "Where did you get these, Mary Alice?"

Each time she took something, Mary Alice grew more afraid. One day she would be caught. She would miscalculate and drop something on the floor, or the clerk would unexpectedly turn around, or Mr. Fishman would happen to walk by. That would be the most terrible thing that could happen. She could see how he would puff up, how his mouth would sputter with outrage. She would be humiliated in front of the whole store. And worst of all, she would never be able to work at her toy department again.

One day it almost happened. She was standing at the stationery counter at closing time again, looking at some paperweights. They were made of plastic, but they looked like glass, and way inside of each one was a perfectly formed and colored seashell. The clerk, a perpetually smiling lady who, even though she was as old as Mary Alice's grandmother, insisted on being called Jenny, was talking to a customer. She looked as if she would be busy for a few minutes. With her eyes Mary Alice picked out the paperweight she liked best—one with a beautiful pure-white cone-shaped shell. Her hand reached out for it, then started to travel back to her open purse. But just at the instant before she would have dropped it in, a voice said, "Those are awfully pretty, aren't they, Mary Alice?"

Mary Alice's stomach turned completely over. She felt her hand start to tremble. She looked up.

Jenny was smiling at her. "We just got them in yesterday. I think they're every bit as nice as the ones they sell for ten dollars in the department stores. Do you think you'd like that one?"

Did she know? Did she suspect? Mary Alice couldn't tell. Her face looked as it always did, open, trusting. No, probably she didn't. Jenny wouldn't believe anyone she knew capable of doing anything like that. Oh, it was lucky it had been Jenny on the stationery counter and not one of the other salesclerks. Or was it so lucky? Looking at Jenny, it suddenly seemed to Mary Alice that she was looking at her grandmother. The smile, the crinkly cheeks, the white wavy hair in a hairnet—somehow it was her grandmother who was standing there watching her.

She had to get away. "Uh—how much is it?" she managed to ask hoarsely. She turned away from that grandmother face, fumbling in her purse for her wallet.

"Only three ninety-eight," replied Jenny. "Oh, you've chosen a lovely one. One of my favorites. Is it for yourself or are you planning to give it as a gift?"

She bubbled on, smiling, forever smiling. Mary Alice tried to force her own mouth into a smile. Then it occurred to her that Jenny's smile was a cover-up. What she was trying to do was keep Mary Alice calm, keep her standing there, and then in a minute she would press the little bell on top of the cash register, and Mr. Fishman would come hurrying over to arrest her.

"I—I better go now," she stammered as she handed Jenny a five-dollar bill.

"Oh, don't you want me to wrap it in tissue for you?" Jenny looked concerned. "They are breakable, you know."

"No—that's all right. Thank you."

Mary Alice took the package and her change and dropped them into her purse. She hurried toward the door, half-expecting at every step to be called back. Even when she was outside the store, feeling the paperweight like a heavy stone in her purse, she waited for someone to come running down the street after her, Mr. Fishman or a policeman maybe. But no one did.

After that she was sure that she would never take anything again. She had learned her lesson. It was over. The sickness had passed. Maybe what her father always said was true. God had been watching over her. He had put Jenny on the stationery counter.

But the sickness had not passed. For two months she didn't take anything. And she never took anything from the five-and-ten again. But the sickness had not passed.

19

"Why did I do it?" Mary Alice asked. She felt an urgency now to talk about it, to understand finally. "What made me take those things? I didn't want to do it. But I couldn't stop myself."

"I know," said the doctor quietly.

"Then why?" Suddenly Mary Alice felt impatient with the doctor's slow careful approach to every subject.

But Dr. Nyquist would not be rushed.

"I wonder if you noticed something about the kinds of things you took from the five-and-ten—the paperweight, the scarf, the perfume."

Mary Alice forced her mind to consider. "Well," she said finally, "they were all—pretty."

"Exactly," said the doctor. "Things that your mother and father might not approve of because they would think them frivolous."

It was true, Mary Alice realized. Still, she didn't quite understand what the doctor was getting at.

"By taking those things, perhaps you were saying to your parents, 'You don't want me to have pretty things, but I want them and I am going to take them.' "

Mary Alice frowned, confused. "But after I took them, I didn't want them."

Dr. Nyquist nodded in agreement. "Because afterward you felt guilty. It was the act of taking something—taking it even when you had the money to pay for it—that was significant. Doing this was a way of expressing anger toward your parents."

It still seemed all topsy-turvy to Mary Alice. But it was beginning to make a little bit of sense.

"There is something else that is interesting," the doctor went on. "You made no attempt to hide the things you had taken. You kept them in your room, even though you knew your mother might easily discover them and ask questions. Have you thought about why you did that?"

Mary Alice hesitated. "Because—do you think it was that I wanted her to find out?"

"I think so—yes. Deep down inside you were hoping to be caught."

"But why?" asked Mary Alice.

"Do you have any idea? What did you think would happen if she did find out?"

"I—don't know. Maybe—maybe she'd know something was wrong."

The doctor nodded, her eyes very earnest. "You were never able to talk to your parents. This was your way, I think, of asking for help."

20

She had thought, after the narrow escape with the paper-weight, that she would never take anything again. And she hadn't for a while. What had made her start again? She had to remember. She had to tell the doctor.

She thought vaguely that it had something to do with boys. It had been in the fall. She could remember the way the September light slanted through yellow-orange leaves, throwing a golden haze over everything, magically transforming the town into a quaint picture-postcard village. She remembered walking to school with Katie through piles of crispy-dry leaves. It was the start of their senior year. Maybe it was just the season, but Mary Alice thought that this year was going to be different, better somehow.

Something was different that fall. Mary Alice suddenly found herself conscious of boys in a way she never had been before. She would see a group of boys playing football on the practice field behind the school, and something about the way they moved, the surging strength and surprising grace of their bodies, sent a shiver up her backbone. Or she would be sitting next to a boy in class, the same boy she had always sat next to in class, and abruptly find herself fascinated by something about him—a faint lingering smell of soap, the way the short hairs grew on the back of his neck, the suggestion of shoulder muscles rippling inside a shirt. It was strange, and a little scary. She felt always aware, in some acutely physical way, of a boy's presence. Not any one boy in particular, but all boys. Was this the way she was supposed to feel? Was this the way Katie had felt last year when she had first started talking about boys all the time? Mary Alice couldn't bring herself to ask her. She was afraid somehow that these new feelings weren't natural, that something very bad was happening to her.

At about the same time another odd thing happened. A boy began to pay attention to her. Richie Folger his name was. He was a stock boy at the five-and-ten. He wasn't at all good-looking really. He was tall and thin, with ears that stuck out and bad skin. And most likely he wasn't too smart either. He had quit school when he was sixteen and was just working at the five-and-ten until he was old enough to join the army. He probably wouldn't be there even that long, because all he did all day was pretend to be busy and joke around with the clerks. Mary Alice was sure that any day now Mr. Fishman would fire him. But the thing about Richie was that he talked to her.

"How're you doing, beautiful?" he would say, passing by with a box of china as she punched in on the time clock. "Better be on your best behavior today. The old man is on the warpath again." And, with a grin, he would draw his hand across his throat in a slitting motion.

"Psst!" He would sidle up to the toy counter, holding something mysteriously behind his back. "Want to buy a diamond ring real cheap?" With a great flourish, he would present her with a box, opening it to reveal an enormous, obviously fake ring. "Well, I told you it was cheap," he'd say. "That's what we sell here—cheap." Then off he would go, looking as if he were on his way somewhere very important, just as Mr. Fishman came walking down the aisle.

"Have a nice weekend," he would tell her on Friday nights, with a knowing wink as if they shared some kind of dark secret. "Not too nice, though. We want to see you in here, bright-eyed and bushy-tailed, on Monday."

Richie teased everyone, even Jenny, the sweet old lady who worked on the stationery counter. But Mary Alice thought he paid more attention to her than to anyone else.

It was because she was closest to his age, of course. That was all it was. Still, when he talked to her, flashing that sudden teasing grin, she would feel herself growing light inside, almost giddy. It was a whole new experience, having someone look at her as if she were pleasing to look at, speak to her as if it were taken for granted that she went out with boys. Mary Alice found, to her surprise, that it wasn't so hard to say something teasing back to him. So this was what it was like, she thought, talking to a boy.

One Friday night at closing time Mary Alice happened to be walking out of the store at the same time as Richie. There was a car parked in front, she noticed, with a girl sitting in it. She didn't think much about it because she was listening to Richie describe how Mr. Fishman had almost caught him smoking a cigarette in the men's room. "You should have seen him, sniffing the air like some kind of old hound dog," Richie said, doing a perfect imitation of Mr. Fishman on the scent of trouble. Mary Alice couldn't help laughing. "Well, here's my old lady. See you around. You be good this weekend now." And he went around to the driver's side of the car and got in.

Mary Alice was stunned. Richie had never mentioned having a girl friend. If he had one, why was he always fooling around, talking to other girls, talking to her? She felt betrayed somehow. It wasn't as if she had expected to go out with him, or wanted to really. He had never appealed to her in that way, she told herself. She couldn't even imagine him in her father's house. But there had been something between them, some sense of undefined possibilities, that was gone now.

Things were different after that. Richie seemed to know it too. He still joked with Mary Alice and the other clerks, but he also started talking about his girl friend. Her name was Marlene, and he had known her for almost two years, and they were going to get engaged before he left for the service. One day he brought in a roll of pictures he had taken of her to show everyone. She was standing next to a barbecue, in some pictures alone and in some surrounded by Richie and another boy holding cans of beer. She looked very young and had stringy-looking hair and sad eyes. "Very nice," said Mary Alice politely and handed them back.

Two weeks after that Richie was fired. Mr. Fishman caught him lighting up a cigarette in the stock room. Mary Alice wasn't there. It wasn't her afternoon to work. But Marge told her the next day when she came in and found a new boy, skinny and scared-looking as a rabbit, wearing Richie's stock apron. "You should have heard the ruckus," Marge said, shaking her head. "Sounded like a cat fight. Customers were perking up their ears all over the store. And then Richie comes running up the stairs with his jacket on, and he gives me a wink and a wave, casual as can be, and I knew that was it."

Mary Alice didn't see Richie after that. He never stopped by the store, like some people did who used to work there. Sometimes she wondered whether he got engaged and joined the army the way he had planned. But she didn't think about him very often. Not about Richie. What she thought about was would anyone ever talk to her again the way he had? Really to her. Would anyone ever take pictures of her standing next to a barbecue?

It was November. The trees were bare now, their branches rattling in the wind that came sweeping through town speaking of winter. Already a few snowflakes had fallen in the night. Mary Alice was startled to see them, glistening in the grass, when she got up. She had never quite gotten used to how long the winters were in West Greenville.

All fall Mary Alice had gone with Katie to almost every game the soccer team had played, sitting on hard wooden bleachers, shivering through the cold, gray afternoons. Katie seemed to have a fixation about soccer players. Now that Carl Schumacher had graduated, she had a crush on this year's captain, Jim Waller. Mary Alice thought she was wasting her time. Jim Waller was so shy that he turned bright red when anyone, even a teacher, spoke to him, and all he was interested in was sports. But she sat there with Katie, watching the boys run monotonously from one end of the field to the other, interrupted only occasionally by a brief burst of action that meant a goal was being scored. It was an odd thing to be doing, Mary Alice thought abstractedly, running around fighting over possession of a grubby gray ball. She found it hard to focus on the game, or care very much which team was winning. She was aware only of bodies running past, compact bodies on hard muscled legs, twisting, turning, bumping each other, falling, rising, flying through the air. It was like some kind of carefully choreographed dance, violent and strangely beautiful in a way that made her ache inside.

One night—it was the night after the last soccer game of the season—Katie called, her voice high, breathless.

"You'll never guess what happened," she gasped.

Mary Alice thought it must have something to do with college. They were both filling out applications, Katie for Michigan State and Mary Alice for Bob Parker University.

But before she could say anything, Katie burst out, "He called!"

Mary Alice could hardly believe it. Jim Waller, who was too shy to talk to anyone, had called. Jim Waller and Katie, going out on a date.

It happened, though. Katie went to the movies with him, and then to the soccer banquet. And suddenly—again—things were different. Even with Katie, things were different.

In some important way Katie wasn't there anymore. Mary Alice and Katie had been the same; the same things had happened to them, and not happened to them. But now, without any warning at all, Katie had gone on without her. She knew what it was like to sit next to a boy in the movies in the dark. She knew what it was like to have a boy drive her home. Of course, Katie told her all about it, all about practically every minute of her dates with Jim Waller, but it still wasn't the same. Mary Alice had been at home watching the Miss Teenage America

Pageant on tv while Katie was sitting next to Jim Waller at the head table at the soccer banquet.

What was wrong with her? Why hadn't it been her instead of Katie that Jim Waller called? She might not be pretty, but she wasn't fat like Katie. *Fat Katie.* Suddenly all kinds of mean hurting thoughts were tumbling through her head. She had sat next to Katie through all those boring soccer games, shivering in the cold, just so that Katie could go out with a boy while she, Mary Alice, stayed home. It wasn't fair. Why had Katie done that to her? Katie was selfish. Fat and selfish. While she, Mary Alice, was thin. She had nice clothes now too. And Richie had even called her beautiful. She remembered he had. Of course he hadn't really meant it, it was just something to say. Still, he wouldn't have called her beautiful if she were ugly, would he? So why hadn't anyone asked her to the soccer banquet?

She kept on wondering about it. She went to school and she couldn't hear what the teachers were saying, her mind was so full of her own thoughts. She looked at the boys, searched their faces not caring whether they saw her staring or not, trying to figure it out. Why didn't any of them see her? Why didn't they talk to her? Could it have anything to do with her father? Once she had heard —or thought she had heard—someone refer to her father's church as "far out." Did they think she was far out too? What was wrong?

She listened to the girls chattering in the halls—even Katie now—about clothes and boys and what they were going to do after graduation, and she felt separated from them by a great distance. Nothing that they talked about seemed to have anything to do with her. No one knew she was there. She was invisible. "Look at me!" she felt like shouting at the top of her voice. But she didn't.

The application for Bob Parker University was all filled out. It sat on the table in the front hall, a fat white envelope, waiting for her father to take it to the post office and send it registered mail. Every time she passed by it, Mary Alice felt weighted down, oppressed. She longed for it to be gone so she could forget it.

On Saturday morning she came downstairs, and before she even reached the bottom, she saw that the envelope was gone. She stood on the last step, looking at the place where it had been, waiting to feel a sense of relief, of calm. But instead she was aware of a sudden queasiness in her stomach, as if the bottom of something had just dropped out. She turned and ran upstairs. She got to the bathroom just in time to throw up.

She was sick all weekend. When she went back to school on Monday, her stomach no longer felt queasy, but it didn't feel normal either. It felt numb. She felt numb all over.

That afternoon after school Mary Alice went to the drugstore on the corner of Main Street and Montrose Avenue, and while the clerk was in the back checking on a prescription, she took a lipstick.

21

"Well, I'll be a monkey's grandmother—it's gone. What did you do with it, toss it out to the birds or flush it down the toilet?"

Mary Alice looked up at the nurse blankly. She couldn't imagine what she was talking about.

"Your lunch. That beautiful club sandwich I brought you a few minutes ago. It's disappeared. Don't tell me Mrs. Cassidy next door came in here and snitched it right off your plate."

The nurse appeared indignant, her arms folded, a dark scowl on her face. Mary Alice gazed at her, trying to figure out whether she was serious or joking. She never could tell.

"I ate it," she said finally, meekly.

"No kidding." The nurse's mouth dropped open, her eyes grew wide, as if she had just witnessed a miraculous event. "Well now, isn't that something. The way you've been picking at your food, I never thought I'd see the day you'd eat a whole sandwich. No, I never did."

She stood there a moment, shaking her head, then seemed to recover enough to go back into action. Picking up the tray from Mary Alice's lap with one hand, she smoothed the sheet with the other, clucking to herself all the while.

"Wait until your mother hears about this. And Dr. Weber. I'm going to go find him right this minute."

And, dishes and heels clicking, she marched from the room.

A second later her head reappeared in the doorway. "Smile pretty now. Company's coming."

Company. Mary Alice tried to think of who it could be. Dr. Nyquist had already been there, and it was too early for her mother and father.

"Mary Alice?"

A girl was standing in the doorway. A girl in a green plaid skirt and matching sweater, carrying a pile of books under one arm. She looked familiar, but for a minute Mary Alice couldn't think who she was.

The girl seemed hesitant about coming in. "Are you—is it okay to visit now?" she asked. "I mean, you weren't sleeping or anything, were you?"

Katie. Of course it was Katie. How could she not have known? It hadn't been that long. Or maybe it had. It seemed as if it had been a hundred years since the accident. Katie's hair was different, shorter, and Mary Alice didn't remember the sweater and skirt at all.

Mary Alice shook her head. "No, it's okay," she said softly.

Katie pushed a chair over to the bed. She didn't seem to know what to do with the books. She started to put them on the bedside table, then changed her mind and finally set them down on the floor next to her chair, looking up with a little half-smile.

"How are you feeling?" she asked.

Katie was thinking the same thing, Mary Alice realized. Of course, she must look different too. Thin, sick, older— something. The accident had changed her. It had changed everything.

"Fine," said Mary Alice. "I feel fine."

The words came out automatically. She didn't know if they were true or not.

"That's quite a contraption to hold up one leg." Katie gestured at all the wires and pulleys over the bed. "But your mother says you're doing very well. She says you're almost better now."

Almost better. She didn't remember anyone telling her that. It couldn't be true. If she were almost better, she would have to go home. She wasn't ready to go home.

Katie was looking down at her hands folded in her lap. She didn't seem to know what to say next.

I ought to help, thought Mary Alice. "How come you're not in school?" she asked. "I mean, isn't there school today?"

Katie appeared relieved at the question. "It's spring vacation this week," she said. "Mom brought me over to have my hair cut, so I thought it would be a good time to bring you the books. You know, the ones your mom talked to Mrs. Marwell about? All the assignments are on a piece of paper in the front." She picked up the top one—her English book, Mary Alice saw it was—to show her. "You're supposed to do as much as you can, and when you're ready I'll bring you some more."

"Thanks for bringing them," said Mary Alice.

"Oh, that's okay," said Katie.

It was the kind of polite talk her mother made with people after church, Mary Alice thought. She couldn't believe it. This was Katie, her best friend.

"How are things at school?" she asked, trying again.

"Pretty good. There are only forty-two school days left until graduation, so everyone's starting to get excited. They say none of the seniors do any work the last month of school, and the teachers don't even say anything."

"Mmmm," said Mary Alice.

It was no use. They couldn't get started, couldn't get it back the way it used to be, when they both would talk about anything that came into their heads without thinking about it first. There were things Mary Alice wanted to ask—she thought she wanted to ask about a boy, but she wasn't quite sure—but she didn't think she should. Things had happened between them; Mary Alice couldn't remember exactly what or how, but it wasn't the same as it used to be. It wasn't simple anymore. It had gotten complicated.

"Well, I guess I better be going," Katie said, looking down at her watch. "Oh, yes, I better. Mom's waiting in the car with Jennifer and Michael. She said to send you her best. So I'll see you in a few days. Tell your mom when you're ready for some more assignments, okay?"

Mary Alice nodded. "Okay."

Katie stood up, walked toward the door. "Oh, I almost forgot. I got my acceptance at Michigan State."

"That's great." Smile, Mary Alice told herself. A smile would be appropriate.

Katie was at the door now. It was too late for the smile. "Well, so long."

"So long," said Mary Alice.

22

It was later in the night, the long hospital night that never seemed meant for sleeping, that she thought of his name. The boy she had wanted to ask Katie about. Alex Benson.

He had come into the class in December, a new boy, just moved into town. She could tell that he didn't come from anywhere nearby, because his clothes were different. He wore sweaters and corduroys, while the other boys wore flannel shirts and jeans. He came from New Jersey, she found out later.

Miss Taylor, her homeroom teacher, asked him to take the empty seat in the back of the second row. There he sat, a new boy whom nobody knew, across the aisle from Mary Alice. Looking down, she could see his left foot, in a thick-soled brown work shoe, stuck out in the aisle. That was all she saw of him the first day. She didn't dare look at his face.

"He's cute," whispered Katie, as they walked down the hall to English.

Mary Alice didn't really know if he was or not. She had only seen his foot, which was big. She guessed he was tall, and she had the vague impression of blondish hair and glasses. That was all. Later she noticed, peeking over when he was absorbed in writing something in a blue notebook, that he had curly hair and a round, almost babyish face. It was as if he had kept the same face he had had when he was four years old, but his body had just gotten longer. He was kind of cute, she decided, in a funny way. Not that it mattered. He wouldn't notice her. He wouldn't talk to her.

He didn't talk to anyone. He seemed shy, or maybe he was finding it hard to get used to living in West Greenville. He sat in the seat next to her, his head bent over the blue notebook, writing something all the time, his foot sticking out in the middle of the aisle.

One day about two weeks after the new boy had come, Mary Alice was sitting in Miss Taylor's study hall doing her French homework when something landed on her book. She looked down to see a tiny folded-up piece of paper. She couldn't imagine where it had come from. It looked as if it had been intended for the wastebasket. She started to brush it onto the floor, but then she noticed the way it was folded, into a precise square. At the same time she had the sudden feeling that someone was watching her. The new boy.

Mary Alice picked up the paper and moved it to her lap. Pretending still to be reading her French book, she unfolded it. Then she looked quickly down. It was a picture of Miss Taylor—a cartoon really, but it looked just like her—sitting at her desk. Only instead of a dress she was wearing a policeman's uniform. Underneath the drawing was written, *All right, don't anyone make a move.*

She had to smile. It was clever. And the drawing was good. So that was what the new boy did all the time, scribbling in his notebook. Mary Alice didn't know what to do. Should she look at him? But then if she did, and he was looking at her, she would feel strange. She might turn red or something. Finally, her eyes on her lap, she folded the paper in half and put it in her French book.

The next day the same thing happened. This time he had drawn Miss Taylor as a bird—a hawklike bird with a sharp beak and big protruding eyes. The caption underneath was, *I've got my eye on you.*

And the day after that he drew a picture of a boy sleeping in a pile of hay. From the curly hair she could tell it was him. Next to it was a note. *Help!* it read. *Save a poor boy from falling asleep right under Miss Eagle Eye's nose*. And under that he had drawn a pattern of two sets of lines—one set going up and down and the other set going side to side—intersecting each other. Mary Alice looked at it. What was that supposed to mean? Was it some kind of code she didn't understand, or the beginning of another drawing? Then she saw an *X* in the lower right-hand corner of the pattern. Tic-tac-toe: That's what it was. He was inviting her to play tic-tac-toe with him.

Mary Alice had never passed notes in class, except once or twice with Katie. She looked to see what Miss Taylor was doing. She was busy talking to one of the girls at her desk. Despite what the new boy had called her, Miss Taylor never paid much attention to what people were doing in study hall.

Mary Alice marked an *O* in the middle square of the tic-tac-toe game. Then she folded up the paper, looked again at Miss Taylor, and tossed it onto the new boy's desk. Quickly she looked down at her math book.

Out of the corner of her eye, she saw the new boy reach down to the floor. The note had missed his desk. How could she be so clumsy? But he was grinning. Slipping the note inside his blue notebook, he unfolded it and wrote something, then passed it back to her.

That was how it began. They played tic-tac-toe until they both knew each other's moves so well that neither of them could win. Then they started playing other games: Hangman and Boxes and another more complicated game that Alex knew that had to do with ships. He was always writing little funny notes and drawing pictures to go with the games, and soon Mary Alice found herself writing notes back. And joking with him after the bell rang for the next class. It was kind of like it had been with Richie, except that this was a boy in her own class, a cute boy, a boy who probably didn't already have a girl friend, since he was new in town.

She found out that Alex hadn't wanted to move to West Greenville, but he had to since his parents were getting a divorce and his mother had brought him and his brother to stay with his grandmother. He was just waiting for school to be over, and then, in the fall, he was going back to New Jersey to live with his father and go to art school. Every other subject in school was a waste of time, he thought. He just wanted to draw.

It got so that Mary Alice wasn't doing any studying at all in study hall. She didn't care though. She didn't even check anymore to see if Miss Taylor was looking when she passed Alex a note. So she was startled one day to hear Miss Taylor call her name.

"Mary Alice."

She had a note from him in her hand. Quickly she crumpled it into a ball.

"Yes?"

"I know that Alex is new and can undoubtedly benefit from your help, but may I remind you both that study hall is for studying?"

Mary Alice felt her face grow hot with embarrassment. She was aware of other kids turning around to look at her and Alex, whispering, smiling. She felt an unexpected burst of pleasure. They were looking at the two of them. Mary Alice and Alex.

"Yes, Miss Taylor," she murmured, her eyes down on her desk.

After class, when she and Katie were getting their books from their lockers, Katie said, "You really like him, don't you?"

"Who?" Mary Alice asked, not looking at her, pretending to be searching for her French book.

"Alex, of course."

She shook her head.

"Come on, Mary Alice, you do."

All at once Mary Alice felt an impulse to tell Katie, to share with her her feelings about Alex as Katie had shared her feelings about Jim Waller. But something held her back. There was a danger in it. In opening yourself to someone else, you left yourself open to being hurt. It was safer not to.

"He's okay," she said, her head still inside her locker. "But you know, he's new, he doesn't know anyone yet. He just wants someone to joke around with in study hall because he's bored with school. That's all it is."

That was probably all it was. But she knew as she said it that she didn't want it to be true. Not this time. This time let it be something more, she found herself praying silently. Please, God. Then she stopped herself. It wasn't right to ask God something like that. If you didn't believe, you couldn't ask favors.

Then it was Christmas vacation. She didn't see Alex for two whole weeks. But she dreamed about him. Two different nights she dreamed that she went out with him, and in one of the dreams they were at the soccer banquet and they were dancing and he was holding her very close. He was holding her and the room was dark and then, right in the middle of the dance floor, he was kissing her. It was so nice—his lips were so soft and he was holding her so tight—that she didn't want it ever to end. She wanted the music to go on forever. And when she woke up, reluctantly, hating to let go of the dream, she felt something strange—a warmness and wetness—down there in that secret part of herself. What did it mean? she wondered, filled with confusion and alarm. "Bad," said a voice inside her head. But why? The dream had been so nice. "No, not nice," said the same voice. "Sinful." It was a voice from some long-ago memory. Her father's voice. "That was a sinful thing for a little girl to do."

Peter was home on vacation, but Mary Alice hardly noticed. She was distracted, lost in thoughts of Alex and the memory of that dream. A couple of times she saw Peter studying her, a puzzled expression on his face. And once he came upon her sitting alone at the kitchen table, gazing out the window and wondering what Alex was doing.

"Are you okay?" he asked.

Mary Alice felt her face redden, afraid he could read her thoughts. "I'm fine," she answered.

"They're not giving you a hard time, are they?" he persisted. "From what I hear, it sounds like Dad is going off the deep end on this Bob Parker business. All this talk about faith-healing and everything."

Mary Alice didn't know what he was talking about. She hadn't heard any talk like that, but she hadn't really been listening lately. Relieved that he hadn't guessed her thoughts, she repeated, "I'm fine."

Then on Sunday morning after church, standing in the vestibule waiting for their parents, he had said to her, "I hear that you've applied to Bob Parker University. Are you sure that's what you want, Mary Alice? Or was it their idea?"

Bob Parker University. The fat white envelope on the hall table. All of that seemed a long time ago.

"I guess I'm going there," she said vaguely. "I don't want to think about it now."

"Really?" His eyes, worried, searched hers.

She nodded, then quickly moved away to get her coat.

Finally Christmas vacation was over. Mary Alice wondered if everything would be the same once she was back in school. Or would Alex have changed his mind about her during the vacation? How would she feel, after that dream, seeing him again?

But it was the same. Coming into her homeroom, seeing him sitting there already in the seat next to hers, solid and real and looking just as good as he had in the dream, she felt a little shiver of excitement. He smiled over at her as she sat down. And later on, in study hall, he passed her a note. At the top he had written: *What I Did on my Vacation.* And under it was listed: *1. Eat. 2. Sleep. 3. Draw.*

He seemed a little happier than before though. He was beginning to know more kids. Mary Alice saw him joking with some other boys in the hall, standing on the corner with them after school, and she felt strange inside, afraid. Don't let him be too happy, she thought. And then, feeling guilty, changed it to Don't let him get to know too many people. Don't let him get to know any girls.

But he didn't seem interested in knowing other girls. He kept sending her notes in study hall and they kept talking after class, and Mary Alice began to allow herself to hope. He would ask her out. Sometime. He was just slow, shy, like Jim Waller. But it would happen.

Early in February there was a big snowstorm. It started in the morning, just a few fine flakes as Mary Alice and Katie walked to school. But then it kept coming down. Mary Alice could see it as she sat in her morning classes, a thick mist of snow obscuring everything from view, making the school seem like a ship adrift at sea. School was almost never canceled because of the weather in West Greenville. They had so much snow each winter everyone was used to it. But at lunchtime it was announced that school would close early because of the storm.

Mary Alice met Katie at her locker.

"I hear there's going to be at least twenty-four inches,"

said Katie. "There won't be any school tomorrow. I'm not taking my books home."

"Me either," said Mary Alice.

Coming out of school, carrying nothing in her arms, Mary Alice felt light, free. She stepped out into an all-white landscape. Snow was everywhere, almost up to her boot tops, drifting over cars and trees, blowing out of the sky in soft clouds. She could hardly see where she was walking, it covered everything so completely. West Greenville was gone. It was as if she and Katie had been set down in some strange new world. A magical world.

So she wasn't surprised when, at the corner, Alex suddenly appeared.

"Hi, girls," he said, grinning. He wasn't carrying any books either. Snow already covered his red-and-black checked jacket and clung to his hair, giving him the look of a walking snowman. "Which way are you heading?"

"Down Main Street," said Katie.

"Me too."

And as easily as that he was walking along between them, stamping snow off his shoes. "New Jersey was never like this. Does it always come down in such large amounts?"

Mary Alice was too conscious of his snow-flecked shoulder looming above her, his arm brushing against hers as they walked, to answer.

"Pretty regularly," said Katie.

He grinned again. He seemed to be in high spirits,

sort of like Katie's dog Grover when he was allowed out to play in the snow. He kept stopping to pick up handfuls of snow, trying to pack them into snowballs, tossing them at trees. "Direct hit!" he would yell when he hit his target. He wandered off the sidewalk into someone's front yard, walking in circles. "Help!" he called. "Can you direct me to the North Pole? I seem to have lost my way."

It was contagious. Soon the three of them were staggering through people's yards, calling to each other, "Help, I seem to have lost my penguin." "Help, I seem to have lost my polar bear." And lying down in snow drifts waving their arms to make snow angels. And tossing handfuls of snow at each other.

When they got to Main Street they found it all closed down, except the drugstore and Bob's Full-Service Gas Station. The bank was closed, and the five-and-ten was closed, and Pearl's Department Store. They walked down the middle of the street, and it was like a ghost town. "Just want you to know," said Alex in a western drawl, "that me and the boys, we run this town. It's no use going to the sheriff, because we're the law around here. You don't believe me, just reach for your six-shooter."

Katie wandered over to look in Pearl's window. "Come here, Mary Alice," she called. "Aren't those sweaters beautiful?"

She pointed to a pile of ski sweaters in soft colors with Scandinavian designs on the neck and sleeves.

"Mmmmm," said Mary Alice. "Pretty."

Alex was next to her. "You ought to have the blue one," he said, "to go with your eyes."

And then he suddenly whirled around, whipping an imaginary gun from an imaginary holster. "Aha! Thought you could slip up on me, did you? Slip up and shoot a man in the back? Well, no one gets the drop on Blackie McGraw, no, sir." And then he was staging a mock gun battle on Main Street, ducking behind parking meters, running from doorway to doorway, shooting in all directions.

Mary Alice and Katie followed him down the street, laughing, until finally, trying to leap on his horse and make a getaway, he tripped over a trash basket. "Ah!" he shouted, clutching his stomach. "Got me!" He lurched all over the sidewalk and finally collapsed, face to the sky, in a pile of snow. "The bad guys lose again."

He lay still for a moment, then jumped to his feet, brushing the snow from his clothes. "Brrr," he said. "My grandmother's not going to like this. Bad boy went out without his boots, and now he's gotten his clothes all wet. She'll probably tuck me in bed with a hot-water bottle."

They walked the rest of the way quietly through the darkening afternoon. The snow was still falling, as if it had no plans ever to stop.

At Katie's house Grover came bounding out to meet them.

"Nice dog," said Alex. "Is he yours?"

"He's not really a dog, he's a furry person," said Katie. "Yes, he's ours."

Alex threw a snowball, and Grover raced after it.

"Well, so long," called Katie, going up the walk. "See you tomorrow, if there's school."

"So long."

Mary Alice and Alex walked on down the street. She was conscious now of being alone with him. Alone, like they were on a date. This was what it was like to be on a date with a boy. Her heart started thumping in her ears. She knew suddenly that this was the moment that everything had been leading up to. He was going to ask her out now.

She was so sure of it that she didn't say anything. She just waited for the words she knew were coming.

They came to a corner. Alex stopped walking. She looked up at him. Now it was going to happen.

"Well," he said, smiling, "I turn off here. So long. See you when we dig out."

Then with a wave he crossed the street and disappeared into the snow.

Mary Alice stood still, not believing it. She waited for something to change, for him to come back. But he was gone.

"So long," said Mary Alice finally.

"I've got to talk to you," said Katie's voice on the telephone the next morning. "Can I come over?"

"Sure," said Mary Alice.

The snow had finally stopped, but there wasn't any school.

A few minutes later Katie was there, sitting on the edge of Mary Alice's bed, looking oddly nervous.

"He called last night," she said.

Mary Alice didn't understand.

"Who called? Jim Waller?"

"No. Alex."

"Alex?" repeated Mary Alice. There must be a mistake.

Katie nodded. "He asked me out," she went on in a rush. "I was so surprised I didn't know what to say. I never expected him to call me. I really didn't."

Mary Alice thought that this wasn't really happening. She heard the conversation as if it were going on at a great distance from her. She wasn't involved. It was a dream, that was all.

"What did you say?" she heard herself ask, calmly, since it wasn't really happening.

Katie looked down. She seemed to be studying the pattern in Mary Alice's rug. "I didn't know what to say. I wasn't sure if you liked him or not. You said you didn't. So I told him"—her voice faded—"yes."

There was a peculiar sound in Mary Alice's ears, a kind of ringing noise, like what you heard when you put a seashell to your ear.

She saw that the other girl, the girl who was sitting on her bed in the dream, was watching her now, her eyes anxious.

"Mary Alice," the girl said, "if you like him I won't go out with him. I'll call him and tell him I can't."

Now something strange was happening to the ceiling

of her room. It seemed to be coming toward her, closing in, crashing down. The world was crashing down.

"No, don't do that," she heard a voice say, a voice she didn't recognize, coming from far away. "You really should go out with him."

23

Things were closing in. Things were crashing down.

Her head ached from trying to hold them back.

She walked to school and she sat in her classes and she walked home again. She didn't remember being there. She was far away.

Sometimes Katie walked next to her.

"I told him I'm not going out with him anymore," she said. "I just went that one time." Katie seemed upset.

Mary Alice didn't know why. She didn't know what she was talking about.

She stood behind the toy counter and she looked at the children who came up to her with money in their hands and expectant looks on their faces. What did they want with her? she wondered. She waited silently for them to go away.

She sat at the dining room table and looked at the food on her plate that she couldn't eat because it all tasted like cotton, and she listened to the voices buzzing around the table. Why did they have to make so much noise? Why was no one ever quiet?

Every once in a while the buzzes became words. There was something about a letter, waiting for a letter from a school about Mary Alice. And Wednesday's Pot-luck Supper and Julia's piano teacher. And the special service. They kept talking about a special service.

Something was going to happen. They all seemed excited about it, especially her father. He spoke in an agitated way, he gestured with his fork, his pale blue eyes burned bright. Vaguely she understood that someone was letting him conduct some kind of special service at the church.

She didn't want to know about it. She wanted to stay inside the little space she was making for herself. A cocoon. She was spinning a cocoon the way the caterpillars that Peter always used to bring home did. She wanted to hide inside it where she would be safe.

But they kept intruding. There was talk about Peter,

whether or not he would come home for the special service. A letter from Peter came. There were frowns, a heavy sigh from her mother. Peter was not coming.

Something else came in the mail. A package. Her mother and Julia watched excitedly while her father opened it, then placed it reverently on a shelf in his study. It was Holy Oil, direct from Bob Parker. Now they could hold the special service. It was going to be this Sunday after church. The Service of Healing.

On Sunday morning Mary Alice lay in bed listening to the sounds of every Sunday morning she could remember: her father shaving in the bathroom, her mother fixing breakfast downstairs, Julia going up and down the stairs changing her dress three or four times. Mary Alice couldn't move. Her arms and legs seemed drained of strength. Her cocoon was attaching itself to the bed now. She would stay there where it was quiet, spinning her cocoon stronger and stronger so that nothing could get in.

"What, Mary Alice, you're not up yet?" Her mother's head was in the doorway, her mother's energy invading the room. "You know this is a special day. Hurry now. Your breakfast is on the table, and we have to leave for the church in twenty minutes."

Slowly, automatically, Mary Alice lifted one leg over the side of the bed and then the other. She walked over to the closet, took something off a hanger, and put it on. She walked downstairs. In the kitchen she stared down at a pile of yellow abused-looking eggs, chewed on a piece of dry toast. Then she was in the car, driving to the church.

There seemed to be more people at church than there usually were, despite a cold drizzling rain. In many of the faces she saw the same look of suppressed excitement that was on her mother's face. Even Julia wore the same expression. Julia will grow up to be her mother someday, Mary Alice thought.

The first part of the service—the regular Sunday service —began. There was singing and a prayer. They stood up and sat down. And then her father read from the Bible. Mary Alice sat next to her mother, half-listening to her father reading, lulled by the familiar yet never quite comprehensible words. She found herself drifting away, as she usually did in church. The voice of her father receded into the background; the church itself began to recede. Lights and colors blurred together; the wooden cross on the white wall above her father's head moved farther and farther away. It was like looking through the wrong end of a telescope. From somewhere in the distance she heard the faint sound of music, soothing, like the rippling of a mountain stream. She was leaving them now, going away, wrapping her cocoon around her like a warm woolly shawl. She was alone. Safe. Unreachable.

But now something was touching her, bringing her back. It was her mother, nudging her to stand for the final hymn. Mary Alice struggled to her feet. Her mother held out the hymn book to her, her strong voice soaring out above all the others nearby.

And then her father was announcing that all those who wished to stay for the special service should move up to the front pews following the benediction.

"Come on, girls," whispered her mother. And a moment later Mary Alice found herself down front, sitting between Julia and her mother in the third row.

"Today we have been given a very special privilege," began her father in a quieter than usual voice. "With the permission of the Board of Elders, and with the assistance of the Bob Parker Foundation, which has provided us with the anointing oil which Bob Parker uses in his healing ministry, this church is holding its first Service of Healing."

Mary Alice stared up at the cross looming behind her father's head. She tried to let his words flow over her, detach herself from what was happening, and drift back to her sanctuary. But something about the juxtaposition of his head and the cross, the somber tone of his voice, held her.

And his eyes, so intense, so close to her now. He had stopped speaking. His eyes roamed the room, taking everything in, missing nothing. Did they see her? Yes, for a long moment they seemed to rest on her. Searching, looking inside. At Mary Alice, his sinful daughter.

He knew, she thought, with a sharp intake of breath. He knew everything about her—the awful craving for things of the world, the lies, the stealing, the bad thoughts about boys' bodies. He knew.

Her eyes dropped to her lap. She bit her lip to still the tumultuous feelings welling up inside her.

His voice boomed out, echoing in the half-empty room.

". . . 'And Jesus saith unto him, I will come and heal him.' "

What was her father talking about? She was listening now, but she didn't understand.

". . . 'And he cast out the spirits with his word, and healed all that were sick.' "

The Service of Healing. The Holy Oil. It couldn't be happening. It couldn't be that he was going to try to do what Bob Parker did, heal sick people through prayer.

". . . And Jesus said, 'Daughter, be of good comfort; thy faith hath made thee whole. And the woman was made whole from that hour.' "

Didn't her father know that only doctors could cure sick people? Why was he doing this? What did he think was going to happen?

She could see beads of perspiration on his forehead, his hands tightly gripping the edge of the lectern as he read from the Bible.

". . . Remember the words of our Lord when he said: 'Ask, and it shall be given unto you; seek, and ye shall find; knock, and it shall be opened unto you. For everyone that asketh receiveth; and he that seekest findeth; and to him that knocketh it shall be opened.' "

It couldn't be happening. But now her father was coming down the steps from the pulpit. And four of the elders who had been sitting in the first pew were rising to stand next to him. Why were they there? Did they really believe in this too? Mr. Pinkerton, the building contractor. Mr. Craig, the insurance man. Did they think they could heal people?

"And now I am going to ask that those of you who wish to receive the prayer for healing come forward. The elders will assist me in administering the Holy Oil."

From the seat right in front of Mary Alice, Mrs. Galbraith rose slowly to her feet, helped by her sister. She had some kind of illness that made her shake all the time. And from the row behind Mary Alice came a mother, Mrs. Hager, carrying a baby. The baby had been born with some sort of heart defect, she remembered. Another old lady with arthritis came hobbling down the aisle. And a man whom Mary Alice had never seen before was pushed up in a wheelchair.

"Those of you who can, will you please kneel on the kneeling bench?" said her father.

Mrs. Hager knelt down, her baby cradled in her arms. It woke up and began crying fretfully. Mrs. Galbraith, her legs trembling violently, lowered herself onto the bench.

"And now let us raise our hearts and our voices in prayer."

Her father lifted his upturned hands toward Heaven. His voice rose.

"O Lord, we beseech thee to look down upon us today and give thy blessing to those among us who are sick, broken in body, mind, and spirit. We ask thee to cast out the illness from their bodies, to mend their broken spirits, to rest thy loving hand of healing upon them that they may be made whole again."

Something odd was happening. Mary Alice felt her head beginning to ache again, as if a great weight were pressing down on it. And then she began to tremble. It started in her legs, then spread slowly through her body.

Now her father's voice was thundering upward.

"O Lord, we pray in thy great and tender mercy, reach down thy healing hand and touch these thy children."

All at once Mary Alice felt a strange urge to stand up, to run forward and throw herself down with those others in front of her father, to receive from him the prayer for healing.

"O Lord, we beseech thee . . . "

She couldn't sit there any longer. The turmoil inside her was too great.

Mary Alice rose to her feet. She stood there, trembling all over, not knowing what was going to happen. Julia was staring up at her, open-mouthed. Her mother reached out to pull her down. But Mary Alice didn't feel her hand.

Stumbling past Julia, she reached the aisle. She looked once more at her father, his arms still outstretched to God, his voice reverberating in the rafters.

Then she turned and ran out of the church.

24

She hadn't been able to stop trembling, even after they found her, sitting hunched up in the back seat of the car.

They took her home and put her to bed.

"It's this terrible weather," her mother said. "She's caught a chill."

And she brought Mary Alice a cup of hot tea and covered her with the afghan her grandmother had knitted for her. But even after Mary Alice had drunk the tea, she continued to shake. She lay there, weighted down by all the blankets piled on the bed, by whatever it was that was pressing down on her head, and every few minutes a new spasm of shivering would come over her.

Something is going to happen, she thought.

All night long she lay there, not sleeping, and the words kept repeating themselves over and over in her pounding head. *Something is going to happen. Something is going to happen.*

In the morning she had stopped shaking, but she still had the same feeling inside her head, as if something were about to burst.

"Well, you don't have a temperature," said her mother, shaking down the thermometer. "Still, I think you'd better stay in bed today. Do you think you'll be all right by yourself for a few hours? I have to help run the senior citizens' lunch today, and your father is going to be out calling on some of the families who received the prayers yesterday. I'll be back about three."

Mary Alice felt something like panic beginning to rise inside her chest. No, she felt like crying out. Don't leave me alone. I can't be alone. Can't you see that? Can't you see that something is going to happen?

But she couldn't say it.

And now the house was empty. Her mother had brought her a bowl of chicken-noodle soup and had left. Julia was at school. Her father was gone. Mary Alice lay in bed looking at the now-cold bowl of soup, listening to the emptiness all around her.

Now, she thought, it was going to happen. She was going to get up from her bed and something was going to happen. It wasn't clear to her exactly what it was. But she couldn't lie in this bed any longer. She couldn't stay in this house any longer. She had to leave.

Very calmly now, as if she were moving in a dream, she got out of bed and put on her clothes. Her school clothes. She didn't know why, but she thought she should wear her school clothes. She combed her hair. Looking in the mirror, she was surprised to see that she looked just the same as she did every morning when she got ready for school. She didn't look as if something was going to happen.

She took the bowl of soup downstairs and poured it out in the sink. Then she rinsed out the dish and spoon and put them in the drainer, neatly, the way her mother did.

Now she was ready. Whatever was going to happen would start now.

Standing there in the kitchen, she thought suddenly of Peter. Why hadn't she thought of him before? What was it he had said to her once a long time ago? If they ever get you down, you can call me. Something like that. That's what she would do. If she could just talk to Peter she wouldn't be alone. And he would stop it—whatever it was—from happening. He was the only one who could. She had to talk to Peter.

She walked over to the telephone and lifted it from its cradle. Carefully she dialed the number that was written on a little slip of paper pinned to her mother's daisy-covered bulletin board. And then it was ringing.

Please, God, she thought, I won't ask for anything else, but let him be there.

The phone was ringing in Peter's room, three hundred miles away. In a moment he would pick it up and she would speak to him and he would tell her that everything was going to be all right. In a moment now it would all be over.

It kept ringing. The sound echoed in her ears until finally she replaced the telephone on its hook. Only Peter could stop what was going to happen. And Peter wasn't there.

She went to the closet and got her coat. She took her purse from the shelf and walked out the front door.

Outside she hesitated a moment, blinking in the bright sun. It seemed odd that the sun would be shining today. Inappropriate. She saw that her father's car was in the driveway. He must have walked, as he often did, to make his calls. The car. Yes, she needed the car. The car was part of what was going to happen.

She took out her keys and got in. Slowly she backed out of the driveway. Then, as if in accordance with some plan she had had in mind all along, she turned left and drove downtown.

When she got to Main Street she saw that, again as if by plan, there was a parking place in front of Pearl's Department Store. Pearl's. That was where she was going. But why was she going there? She thought vaguely that it had something to do with a sweater. Yes, that was it. The sweater.

She walked inside. The store was empty. There were just three salesladies standing together talking in the dress department. Mary Alice walked over to the sweater counter. And immediately she saw it, inside the case, right on top. The blue sweater with the Scandinavian design on the neck and sleeves.

"May I help you?" One of the salesladies broke away from the others and came toward her.

Mary Alice nodded. "I'd like to see that sweater," she said. Her voice sounded husky, as if she had, in fact, caught a chill.

The saleslady took the sweater out of the case and laid it on top of the counter. "It's a lovely color," she said.

Mary Alice looked down at it. It was a lovely color. Pale blue, soft as the sky. "You ought to have the blue one," she seemed to hear someone saying, "to go with your eyes."

She put her hand inside the plastic bag to touch the sweater. It felt as soft as it looked, soft as a cloud. It was beautiful. She stood there looking at it, touching it.

"Take your time," the saleslady said, and ambled back to where her friends were standing.

Everything about the sweater was right. It was meant for her. So soft. And it went with her eyes. When she wore it, he would see her. When she wore it, everything would be different. She couldn't wait to put it on.

Picking up the sweater, holding it tight against her, Mary Alice walked toward the door.

"Miss!" she heard someone call. "Wait a minute, miss."

Mary Alice kept walking.

"Miss, come back! You didn't pay for that."

Mary Alice looked back. Who was the saleslady talking to? She seemed upset. What was the matter with her?

"She took the sweater," the saleslady was saying to someone. "Call the manager."

Mary Alice looked down. The sweater.

Suddenly her heart was beating wildly, pounding in her ears. She started to run.

She ran out of the store. There was the car, right in front. If she could just get to the car. But someone was coming after her. They were chasing her.

She fumbled with the door and got in, dropping the sweater on the car floor. Any second now they would burst out of the door after her. She had to hurry.

She tried to put the key into the ignition, but her hand was shaking so that she dropped it. She picked it up, tried again. The car jerked forward, bumping the fender of the car in front. It flashed through her mind that this was ridiculous, like a scene from some dumb tv movie. And then she was pulling away from the curb, driving much too fast down Main Street.

They were coming after her. They must be right behind her. The police. The store would have called the police. In a moment she would hear the shriek of a siren, see the flashing red lights in her rear-view mirror.

She was almost out of town now. The houses looked so quiet here, as if no one were living in any of them. The only sign of life was a woman with a green scarf on her head walking along the sidewalk pushing a baby carriage. How could she walk along so peacefully, not knowing what was happening to Mary Alice? If only somehow Mary Alice could change places with that woman.

But now the woman pushing the baby carriage was out of sight. And Mary Alice was leaving West Greenville. She dared a look in the rearview mirror. No one was behind her. No flashing red lights. Did she hear a siren somewhere in the distance? Or was the siren inside her head? She wasn't sure. Anyway, she had to keep on going.

She drove and she drove. Far out of town. Past the other towns where she and Katie used to go to look at houses. She was on a road she had never been on before, a country road that twisted and turned past winter-brown fields rimmed with melting snow, faded gray barns, an occasional deserted-looking store with a gas pump out front. There was no one behind her now. She was sure of it. No flashing lights. No sirens. She had left them behind.

But still she kept driving, fast, the fields falling away on either side as she hurtled on, cutting through the landscape like a knife slicing through butter. Forward, always forward, on to somewhere else, rejecting where she was before she could even see it, not able to see it because she was going so fast.

Then the road she had been on ended abruptly. A new road lay ahead. She could turn either left or right. She wondered momentarily what direction she had been going—north? west?—and where this new road would take her. But it didn't matter. She turned right.

The new road was like the old one. Narrow, hilly, winding. She passed scrawny-looking cows in a muddy barnyard. A newly built ranch-style house sitting alone in a field.

The sky was gray now. It was getting dark. She must have been driving for hours. She peered again into the rearview mirror. There was nothing behind her. No other cars. No lights coming on in farmhouses or stores. No other people. No one but her on that gray winding road.

Alone. Why was she alone? What was she doing here? Where was she going?

She glanced again in the rearview mirror, and this time she saw something. Two eyes, dark, burning, staring at her. Accusing eyes. Eyes that pierced right through her. Why could she never get away from those eyes? Her father's eyes.

No, they were her own eyes.

She had to get away from them. She stepped on the accelerator, and the car leaped forward. Down the road through the gray dusk she sped, around curves, up and down hills. Coming from nowhere. Going nowhere. Faster and faster.

Just ahead she saw something on the road. Something dark, wet. The road was wet from melting snow. Slow down, she told herself. It's slippery. You'll skid. What does it matter? she asked herself. The car seemed to be traveling on its own momentum now. It was out of her control. What would happen would happen.

Then, suddenly, the road curved sharply left. She stepped down hard on the brake pedal. The car swerved wildly.

If only she could hold it on the road. Help me, God, please help me, she heard herself praying.

And then she felt the car leaving the road, skidding, out of control.

The earth was spinning, over and over. Upside down, inside out. Everything was black and spinning.

And Mary Alice was falling. Slowly falling, down and down and down through vast unending space.

25

Now the room was full of sunlight. It streamed through the curtains, which the nurse had opened wide. It fell on the bottom of the bed, forming a neat triangle over Mary Alice's feet. It touched the chair where the doctor was sitting.

The doctor had been quiet for a long time.

Inside Mary Alice's head was a question. She had been hearing it over and over.

"Now what is going to happen?"

She spoke the words aloud.

Dr. Nyquist looked over at her. "After you go home, you mean?"

Mary Alice nodded.

"It will be soon, I think," the doctor said. "Your leg is healing nicely. In a few days you will be out of traction. You will have to be in a cast for a while, but you'll be able to get around on crutches. I am sure Dr. Weber will say you can go back to school. You have missed five weeks of classes, which is a long time. But if you work hard, I feel sure you will be able to graduate with the rest of your class."

Mary Alice felt her stomach tighten. "I don't know—" She hesitated. "I don't know if I can go back to school."

The doctor nodded. "It will be hard. It will seem to you that you have been away far longer than five weeks. But I think you can manage it. Your father has talked to the store manager, and they are not-going to press charges. So no one at school will know what happened, just that you were in an automobile accident."

Mary Alice felt a sense of relief. But still her stomach was tight, twisted.

"My mother and father—they know. I don't think— I'm not sure if I can live at home."

Again Dr. Nyquist nodded in agreement. "It may not be easy," she said. "But you won't be alone. Your brother Peter is coming home soon for the summer, I believe. And you and I can continue to talk, in my office. If we do continue, it might be a good idea—both for you and your parents—to think about paying for the sessions yourself. From the money you make at the five-and-ten or whatever job you get for the summer. It would be a way of beginning to be independent."

"But—" Mary Alice looked up at the doctor. There was still something that she had to know that the doctor had not told her. "If I live at home, will it be the same?"

Dr. Nyquist looked back at her, her eyes clear blue, steady. "That is up to you," she said.

Up to you. That was it. It was up to her. Not the doctor, not Peter, not Katie, if Katie was still her friend. Not anyone else. They would be there, but that was all. She was the one who would have to make things happen.

Her eyes dropped down to the bedspread. So worn, so drab, so familiar. Mary Alice wished suddenly that she never had to see it again.

She took a deep breath.

"I—I don't want to go to Bob Parker University."

There it was. She had said it. Mary Alice raised her eyes to see the doctor's reaction. Dr. Nyquist said nothing, but it seemed to Mary Alice that a smile flickered briefly across her face.

"But if I don't go there, what will I do? It's too late to apply to any other colleges. If I don't go to Bob Parker, I will have to get some kind of job and live at home."

The room was silent for a moment.

Then the doctor said quietly, "That is one alternative.

But there are others. It is true that it's late to apply to other schools. I'm not sure, though, that it's too late. It's possible that you might still be accepted somewhere. There is the state university. And there are a couple of community colleges not too far away that you might look into. Your brother may know of other schools. Or another possibility might be to think of entering college a semester late, in January."

Possibilities. Yes, she could see that there were possibilities. If she were strong enough to look for them.

Dr. Nyquist seemed to sense what she was thinking.

"Of course you will have to tell your parents that you are not going to Bob Parker University."

Mary Alice was aware again of her stomach, twisted into a hard knot inside of her. Would she ever come unknotted?

"I am afraid," she said, her voice a whisper.

"I know," said Dr. Nyquist softly. And then, "Do you remember that I asked you a few days ago to imagine yourself saying No to your father. And I asked you to think about the worst thing that could happen?"

Mary Alice nodded.

"Why don't you try it now?"

Mary Alice raised her eyes again and saw for certain this time that Dr. Nyquist was smiling. In that smile something seemed to flow from the doctor to her, a current, faint but steady. Was it possible for the doctor to give her just a tiny portion of her strength?

Mary Alice closed her eyes. In her imagination she went back again to that night at the dinner table, months ago. The smell of pork chops, her mother chattering away about the Flower Committee meeting, Julia playing with her mashed potatoes and gravy, her father chewing silently on his food, engrossed in thoughts of his Sunday sermon.

And then her mother saying, "Mary Alice has been wondering if she should apply to some other schools besides Bob Parker University."

And her father, pulling himself out of his thoughts, looking over at her in surprise.

Now was the moment.

This time she wouldn't wait for her father to reply. She wouldn't look down at her dinner plate, hesitating, wavering. She would look straight at him and say, calmly and firmly, "I'm sorry, but I'm not going to Bob Parker University."

Then would come the hardest part. The worst thing that could happen. The way they would look at her. Her mother's puzzled face, her father's eyes.

Yes, that was the worst thing. Her father's eyes.

Hurt, angry eyes. Cold as marble. Unbending as steel. Filling her with doubt. Filling her with guilt.

But this time Peter would be at the table too.

And Dr. Nyquist. She could talk to Dr. Nyquist.

But her father's eyes.

Mary Alice opened her own eyes.

Dr. Nyquist was still there, sitting quietly in her chair, waiting. Sun was still streaming into the room.

Mary Alice looked past the doctor, at the curtains, stirring slightly in the breeze. For a long moment she gazed into them, fearful of what she would see staring back at her.

But all she saw there was a rabbit, standing on its head.

Jean Van Leeuwen grew up in Rutherford, New Jersey, where her father was a Congregational minister for many years. A graduate of Syracuse University, she worked as a book editor before moving to Chappaqua, New York, with her husband, a computer-systems designer, and their two young children. She now devotes as much time to writing as she can and also teaches a writers' workshop.

Ms. Van Leeuwen is the author of a number of children's books. She enjoys gardening and photography.